JAKE and LILY

ALSO BY
JERRY SPINELLI

SMILES TO GO
MANIAC MAGEE
WRINGER

JERRY SPINELLI

JAKE

and

LILY

BALZER + BRAY

An Imprint of HarperCollins*Publishers*

Balzer + Bray is an imprint of HarperCollins Publishers.

Jake and Lily
Copyright © 2012 by Jerry Spinelli
All rights reserved. Printed in the United States of America.
No part of this book may be used or reproduced in any manner
whatsoever without written permission except in the case of brief quotations
embodied in critical articles and reviews. For information address
HarperCollins Children's Books, a division of HarperCollins Publishers,
10 East 53rd Street, New York, NY 10022.
www.harpercollinschildrens.com

Library of Congress Cataloging-in-Publication Data is available.
ISBN 978-0-06-028135-9 (trade bdg.)
ISBN 978-0-06-028136-6 (lib. bdg.)

Typography by Carla Weise
12 13 14 15 16   CG/RRDH   10 9 8 7 6 5 4 3 2
❖
First Edition

DOUBLE THANK-YOUS TO:

Queen of the Rails, Eileen Oshinsky

Our cyberwizard, Dottie Lieb

My editor, Donna Bray

My copyeditor, Kathryn Hinds

My wife, Eileen

**TO THE KIDS,
BOTH GRAND AND GREAT-GRAND,
WHO HAVE ARRIVED SINCE THE LAST LIST:**

Wesley

Lulu

Oli

Vika

Kolia

JAKE

and

LILY

Intro

I'm Jake Wambold.

I'm Lily Wambold.

This is the story of our lives.

Life.

Whatever. We're taking turns.

For this intro, we're taking turns on lines.

Like, this line is me (Jake).

And this line is me (Lily).

Then we'll take turns on chapters.

We don't know how many chapters this book will have.

But even if it had a million chapters,
we couldn't tell you the whole story.

Because

well

uh

it's hard to explain.

You'll just have to take our word for it.

Especially the beginning. You might think
it's weird.

Forget might. *They're* gonna *think it's weird.*

Anyway, first you're going to hear from me
(Jake) because

Don't say it.

I'm older.

Ha!

That's why I did the first line too.

Whoopee.

But that's not the cool thing.

Finally he's off who's older, who's first.

The cool thing is, we can do this without looking at

what each other is writing.

We *could* show each other, but we don't
have *to.*

I told you you might think it's weird.

Gonna.

Let's get started before we weird them away.

*Not so fast. Tell them how much
older you are than me.*

Here we go.

Tell them.

Eleven minutes. Happy?

Eleven measly minutes.

First is first.

*Because of eleven minutes,
I'll be in second place my whole life.*

Boohoo.

One more thing.

So you probably figured it out by now. We're not
just brother and sister. We're

twins!

(That last word was done by both of us.)

Jake

Light!

Hurricane of light coming at me. Swallows me. I am blinding, screaming light. It's gone. I'm still here. Dark. Cool. Silent.

Below me railroad tracks gleam in moonlight. Cool, rough cement on my bare feet. Somewhere a clock strikes. I count. Three. In the morning? I'm in my pajamas. Where am I? Why aren't I in bed? Am I dreaming?

I smell pickles.

I am not alone. I hold out my hand.

Lily

Our hands touch. Everything is okay.

"I just had a dream," he says.

"What about?" I say.

"I was standing down there"—he points to the tracks—"and there was a bright light and—"

"—and a train went through you!"

He looks at me. "How did you know?"

"I had the same dream."

We look at each other. We look up the tracks. There is no sign of a train.

"Maybe we're still dreaming," he says. "Poke me."

I poke him.

"Harder."

I poke harder.

He squeals, "Ow!"

"Tickle me," I say.

He tickles me, in my worst spot.

I howl.

"We're not dreaming," he says.

"Not anymore," I say.

"Where are we?" he says.

We look around. Railroad tracks. Benches. Wooden posts prop up a roof that brims out over the concrete platform we stand on. A dim mist of light from the street behind.

"I think it's the train station," he says.

"What are we doing at the train station?" I say.

"How did we get here?" he says.

We stare at each other.

"Sleepwalk?" I say, not believing myself.

"Sleepwalk?" he says. "I don't sleepwalk."

"Me neither," I say.

We stare into the darkness. Crickets shake their rattles.

"Well," I say, "I guess we do now."

We're quiet some more. Thinking. Or trying to. How do you think about something you don't understand?

"Lil?" he says.

"Huh?"

"In the dream?"

"Yeah?"

"Did you smell something?"

"Yeah."

"What?"

"You say it."

"Let's both say it."

"Pickles!"

More silence. A distant voice shouts but I can't make out the word.

"Jake?"

"Huh?"

"Are you scared?"

"No."

"Me neither."

Silence. Night.

"Jake?"

"Huh?"

"When the train came?"

"Yeah?"

"Did you feel something?"

"What do you mean?"

"*Feel*. When the train came, did it *feel* like something?"

"Yeah. It felt like a train coming."

"What else?"

"Huh?"

"What *else*? What else did it *feel* like?"

He looks at me. His eyes go wide. He smiles. "Home."

Jake

That's how it started. I said "home" and my sister smiled and then for no good reason we both started giggling, just standing there giggling on the train platform in the middle of the night.

We left the station. We started walking down the street. Talking . . .

Lily

and talking . . .

Jake

and talking.

We were only six then, but we were old enough to know something amazing had just happened. We had both sleepwalked to the *same place* at the *same time—on July 29, our birthday!*

And there was more—the train station, the train. All our lives we had been hearing the story: we were born on a famous train, the California Zephyr. Our parents already knew they were going to have twins, but we weren't supposed to come out for another month, so Mom figured they had plenty of time to go to San Francisco for Uncle Peaceboy's wedding. They took the cross-country train instead of flying so Mom could be more comfortable. After the wedding, on the train back, we were born to the surprise of everybody. In the Moffat Tunnel. The Moffat Tunnel is over six miles long and goes under the mountains in Colorado. Personally, I was perfectly happy to wait till Mom got home to be born. But Lily, of course, being Lily, she couldn't wait. I swear if I concentrate real hard, I can remember her inside our mother pushing me from behind. So into the world we came, first me (I'll say it for her: ha!), then Lily, in a compartment in a sleeping car. By the dark windows of the Moffat Tunnel. And pickle smell. Because it happened so fast that Dad came rushing from the club car, where he had just bought and taken his first bite out of a big fat dill pickle. There was no doctor, just Dad and the conductor and two waitresses from the dining car.

So now we walked along the night-lit streets and talked about that and boggled over it and nudged each other and giggled at the amazement of it all. And we started to remember things, things that up till then we hadn't thought much about. Like the time Lily was crying, "I'm stuck! I'm stuck!" only she wasn't. She was sitting on the living room floor with a coloring book. It was *me* who was stuck.

Mom found me in the backyard. My foot had gotten caught beneath the fence and I couldn't pull it loose.

Like the time I yelled "Stop!" and Lily heard me and stopped—just as she was about to chase a ball into the street when a car was coming. No big deal, maybe you're saying, except at the time I was at the dentist—*five miles away.*

Lily

As if that explains everything.

As usual, Jake misses the point. He skims the top off things. Sure, what *happened* was that we both sleepwalked to the train station at the same time. And had the same dream. And talked and talked. But that was just the cherry, the whipped cream. Down deep with the hot fudge and ice cream was what *else* happened. What *really* happened. Which was this: we became ourselves. I know, it sounds weird. But it's like, on the train in the Moffat Tunnel that night, not quite all of us was born. I mean, it looked like all of us was born. But something was missing. The knowing. We didn't *know* who we were. Not really. (The important word there is *we*.) We just went along with the program for the first six years, being but not knowing ourselves. Being "twins." To everybody else: adorable, mysterious twins. To ourselves: Duh, so what's the big deal?

And then we awoke that night hand in hand at the train station, and it's like the *rest* of us was finally born. We knew. At last we *knew*. We saw ourselves like everybody else saw us. It suddenly hit us: we're different!

It's like a beautiful present had been sitting there for six years and we never noticed it and then finally we did and we tore it open and . . . *wow!* The present was *us*.

So what exactly is it that we finally knew?

Well, we knew that not everybody can hear their brother from five miles away. We knew that not everybody yells, "I'm stuck!" when it's happening to somebody else.

Okay, that's what we knew about everybody else, but what about *us*? What did we finally know about *us*?

We couldn't say—we could only feel—because there were no words. It's like, whatever it was, it existed on the other side of words. So if you were following us on the way home from the train station that night, you wouldn't have heard regular, full-sentence talk. All you would have heard were scraps, like "Did you see . . . !" and "What a fantastic . . . !" and "Do you believe . . . !" And that's about all. Because the rest of the talk was happening between our heads, not our mouths.

What an amazing night, the night we unwrapped ourselves. Before we knew it, Jake pointed to the sky and said, "Look—it's morning!" We had been circling our block all night—two six-year-olds in July in pj's and bare feet. We raced for home. The front door was wide open. We ran to the kitchen, grabbed cereal boxes and bowls. We were just starting to eat—hard to do when you're gulping giggles—when Mom came down.

She nearly fainted. "What are you two doing up? You're never up this early."

"We're too excited to sleep," Jake said.

"It's our birthday!" I said.

Jake

Our birthday party was in the backyard. Some cousins were there plus a couple of neighborhood kids. Dad grilled hot dogs and hamburgers. The cake had blue and pink candles. We both blew them out at once. Well, I blew. Lily burped. It was her first public burp. Everybody laughed, so ever since then she thinks she's the world's greatest burper. She can burp on command. She practices.

Dad took our picture as we stood next to a step-ladder. He said he was going to do it every year on our birthday, to show how we're growing up the ladder.

For her present, I gave Lily a model train engine. (Mom paid for it.) Lily didn't even know she wanted it, but I did. I wrapped it in a paper bag. When I gave it to her, she screeched, "A train!" Mom said, "No fair, you peeked." But she didn't peek. She didn't have to.

Lily gave me a stone. I was already collecting stones by then. She must have found it at the creek, because it was worn smooth as glass. It was the size and shape of a robin's egg, gray with thin pink lines through it. I still have it.

Every year our parents give us tools. That year it was a tape measure for Lily, a ball-peen hammer for me. Mom and Dad have their own construction business. They build and renovate houses. They don't believe in buying stuff you can make. Their motto is "If you want it, make it."

One of the kids at the party was a mystery. Nobody knew him. He said his name was Bump. Turned out he lived up the street. Bump Stubbins. He saw the party going on and invited himself. Nobody had the heart to tell him to scram. He had a Mohawk haircut.

After we opened our presents, I saw him walking away. A couple minutes later he came back with a big grin and said, "Happy birthday," and gave me a stone. A muddy, ordinary-looking stone. I was thinking if I washed off the mud maybe it would look pretty neat. But Lily wasn't fooled. "That's stinky," she said. She grabbed the stone from my hand and threw it into the next yard. She snarled at him, "Don't ever give my brother a stinky stone again." Already she didn't like Bump. She turned to Dad. "Daddy, kick him out. Nobody invited him." Dad just laughed and said, "Now be nice, Lily. You're the birthday girl."

That was the day we found out we couldn't play hide-and-seek. There were no good places to hide in the yard, so us kids were let into the house. "You can hide anywhere downstairs," my dad told us. "But no upstairs."

When Lily was It, I hid in the back of the closet in the mudroom. As soon as Lily reached one hundred, I heard her call, "Give it up, Jake! I know you're in the mudroom!"

When I was It, Lily cheated. She sneaked upstairs. My sister cheats a lot. Which is no big deal, because she's so bad at it she doesn't fool anybody. She lies too. Anyway, when I finished counting and opened my eyes, I knew exactly where she was. "Lily!" I called. "Come down from behind the shower curtain!"

"Rats!" I heard her growl.

As she came stomping down the stairs, Mom and Dad were gaping at me boggle-eyed.

Lily

Jake got one thing right—I didn't like Bump from the start. But more about that meatball later.

Because we had been awake since three o'clock in the morning that sixth birthday, we went to bed right after dinner. The last thing I said to Jake was, "Should we tell Mommy and Daddy?" Jake said, "Not yet."

Years later *not yet* is still going on.

For a long time our parents didn't have to tell us to go to bed. We couldn't wait to be alone in the dark so we could giggle and talk about our amazing secret. Our talk happened in an up-and-down direction because we had bunk beds then. Of course I was on top.

It's like the secret was our new toy. But it

wasn't an easy toy to play with. I think at first we thought we were magicians or wizards. We figured we had powers. "Maybe we're superheroes," Jake said one day. "Yeah," I said, "maybe this is what superheroes are like when they're little kids." We were actually serious. Well, not serious enough to try flying off our roof. But serious enough to make up magic words and paint a stick gold and convince ourselves it was a magic wand. We tried to make the teakettle talk. We tried to make daggers spring from our fingernails. We tried to set the sofa on fire by staring at it. Nothing worked. Shoot, we couldn't even make a chair walk across the room.

We tried to wizardize somebody else. Bump Stubbins started coming around on his Wonder-Wheels the day we got our own WonderWheels. We would go riding off down the sidewalk and there he was, pedaling along with us. He kept turning off and saying, "This way! This way!" but we never followed and he had to turn around and catch up with us. One day I had enough. I pointed the gold stick at him and said, "Moozum!" three times and concentrated as hard as I could. At first I pictured his arms falling off. I peeked and saw that wasn't happening, so I settled for just making him disappear. But there he was, as visible as ever and even more annoying because he was smirking at me.

So we figured out pretty quick that whatever power we had—we still didn't have a word for it—was just between the two of us. And we had more to learn. One day I heard a thump in the dining room. Jake was on the floor, ready to cry, rubbing the back of his head. "What happened?" I said. "I let myself fall backward," he sniveled. "I thought you would catch me."

Another time I was in the backyard and I wanted Jake to come out and play, so I closed my eyes and I concentrated on his name: *Jake . . . Jake . . . come to me.* My eyelids were getting sore, and still he wasn't coming. I found him in the basement playing with Mom and Dad's tools.

I would think about cupcakes and say, "What am I thinking about?" and he would say "donkeys" or "Bugs Bunny"—anything but cupcakes.

Every day we said to each other, "What are you thinking? What are you thinking?" We never knew. Weeks went by. Months. Nothing happened.

We tried playing hide-and-seek. We couldn't find each other. We were back to being ordinary run-of-the-mill twins. It's like our powers had tricked us. Teased us. Made us feel special, then backed off.

"Maybe it was a phase," I said.

"What's a phase?" said Jake.

I had heard our parents use the word. "I think it's, like, when you outgrow something."

Jake's mouth pouted. "I don't want to outgrow it."

"Me neither," I said. Our heads came together and we were sad. We went to bed sad.

But on our next birthday—our seventh—we woke up in the middle of the night. At the train station. To a blinding light. And the smell of pickles.

Jake

So that's how it went from then on. Every birthday night—July 29—there we were, at the old train station, in our pajamas, waking up from the same dream, the blinding light of the oncoming train, the smell of pickles. We weren't worried about our power ditching us anymore. We knew it was there. We knew it would come and go on its own schedule, not ours.

I was happy to call it our "thing" or "power." But that wasn't good enough for Lily. She kept saying it had to have its own one-of-a-kind name. Then one school morning I felt something pressing my nose. I opened my eyes. Lily's face was hanging upside down from her upper bunk. "Goombla," she said. I just stared. "It's goombla." I knew exactly what she was talking about. We finally had a word for our special thing. *Goombla.* I just didn't like her timing. It was five o'clock. "Go to sleep," I growled, and turned over.

Every birthday I gave Lily a train car. Every year she gave me a stone. But there were no more parties at the house. Lily was afraid Bump Stubbins would show up again, so she begged our parents to do our birthdays at The Happy Hippo.

One thing was the same for every birthday: we got twin presents from Grandpa Dooley (our mom's dad). We call him Poppy. Poppy and Grandma Dooley lived in California. Dad says they were flower children left over from the seventies. They were hippies. They lived over a garage and drank green tea, and Grandma wore a flower in her hair every day like it was still the seventies. In pictures we saw, Poppy's hair was as long as Grandma's. The only shoes they had were sandals.

Grandma died trying to save the redwoods. She was perched in a giant redwood two hundred feet up for eight days and refused to come down until they stopped cutting down the trees. But something broke up there and she fell. And then, in a way, so did Poppy.

"Poppy went off the deep end," Mom and Dad told us. He tried to be a regular person. He got a haircut. And socks. He got a job in a supermarket and then an office and then a bank. But he just couldn't do it, not without Grandma. One day he walked out of the bank and never came back. He walked clear out of California. He was gone by the time of Uncle Peaceboy's wedding and our birth on the train. Nobody heard from him until a strange box came to the house the day before our second birthday. It was from Mexico and inside it were two sombreros. Even though they were kid-sized they were still too big for us, but we wore them anyway, down over our faces, because we loved them so much.

Poppy sailed to every continent. He worked on freighters and tankers. Every birthday a box arrived from a different country. We got bolos from Argentina, tiny silver elephants from India, emu feathers from Australia, voodoo masks from Haiti. The two gifts were always identical.

"Why doesn't Poppy ever come see us?" We were always asking that. The only answer we ever got was, "He's trying to find himself." That made no sense. When we got old enough to have our own email address, we kept sending messages to his BlackBerry: "Hurry up and find yourself so you can come see us." He always answered us, but the only thing that showed up on our porch was a birthday box every July 29.

Bump Stubbins kept showing up too. Lily kept telling him to get lost. He was a real clown. He would crash his bike into a telephone pole. He would pretend to walk into a wall. He would reach into his nose with the tip of his tongue. For a while there he had a new act every day. I guess he figured if he could make Lily laugh, she would let him join us. But she wouldn't even look at him. Me? I just thought he was funny.

He was especially funny the day Lily and I were on the porch wearing our sombreros and practicing our Mexican: "*Si si!*" and "*Muchos gracias!*" Bump comes along, and before you know it he snatches my hat and plops it on his own head. I was mad at first, but when I saw how funny he looked, all I could do was laugh. But Lily went after him. He jumped down from the porch and started running.

That's the day he found out how fast Lily is. She caught him and grabbed for the hat. But it didn't come right off because it had a string that went under the chin, and when she pulled at the hat the string caught his neck and he jerked to a stop. Lily grabbed the hat and brought it back to me. Bump staggered home whimpering, and we figured that was that.

That day after dinner Bump showed up with his mom. She showed our parents the mark on his neck. And here's where it got surprising for Mrs. Stubbins. Before she had a chance to say anything else, Lily squeezed out from between Mom and Dad and piped up, all cheery, "I did it!" Mrs. Stubbins first looked shocked, then disappointed because she didn't have a chance to complain or accuse anybody. She glared at Lily, glared at me, glared at our parents. "Well," she said, "I hope you're going to punish her for choking my son."

"Oh, we will," our father said.

I guess Bump still wasn't satisfied, because then he snarled at Lily, "And you ain't *twins* neither. Twins look exactly *alike*."

Lily went for him, but Dad caught her by the

shirt collar. He smiled at Mrs. Stubbins. "We have it covered."

After Bump and his mom stomped off, Dad said one simple word to Lily: "Room."

Lily put a grump on her face and slumped upstairs. She wasn't going to our room but to the Cool-It Room. Lily will explain that in a minute.

See, what Mrs. Stubbins didn't know is that Lily confesses. (I already told you that she lies, but she never lies when the question is, "Did you do it?" She steals my pumpkin seeds but never denies it.) Confessing is very rare among kids. And she didn't mind getting punished, especially when punishment was the Cool-It Room.

Lily

I loved the Cool-It Room. Jake knew it but our parents didn't. They saw me grumping and slumping and they thought I hated it. I was like Brer Rabbit in the briar patch. *No! No! Anything but that! Pleeeeeze don't throw me in the Cool-It Room!*

The Cool-It Room was on the third floor. Still is. It's a big old house we live in, and most of the third floor is a dusty attic loaded with junk from renovated houses. But there's also a door that leads to a little room. Dad says I first got sent there when I sawed Jake's foam-rubber football in half because I was mad at him. I guess I couldn't stay out of trouble, because I kept getting sent to the attic dungeon, which Dad started calling the Cool-It Room. Jake started getting sent up too, but only about once for every ten times for me. We were always sent up with a cooking timer. Dad set the timer according to "the horribleness of the crime," as he used to say. When the timer went *ping!* we could come out.

Dad was a genius. He knew that the worst punishment for a kid is boredom. And that's what the Cool-It Room was: B-O-R-I-N-G. Ceiling, floor, four walls—it was nothing but six bare sides. So I don't blame Dad for figuring I'd be good just to stay out of there. But it just wasn't in the cards, I guess. I kept messing up, Dad kept pointing: "Lily—Cool-It Room." So I figured as long as I was going to be spending a lot of time there, I might as well make myself comfortable. I started sneaking stuff from the attic into the room. Braided rag rugs. A white wicker rocking chair. A bench. Cushions. Books. Games. And my carnival prize, Joe the grinning gorilla. Whenever I wasn't in the room, Joe got to sit in the rocking chair.

It got to be so nice in there I started getting in trouble just so I'd get sent up. Even Jake liked it. Which he didn't at first. He would just mope and grumble and stare at the timer till it went *ping!* But after I fixed up the room, we did coloring books (when we were little) and Monopoly and Old Maid. We had burping contests, which of course I always won. And we played tic-tac-toe on the walls. Those were some of the happiest times of my life, playing games and writing on the walls of the Cool-It Room with Jake. Sometimes we kept playing after the *ping!*

So yeah, I confess. So yeah, I get in trouble. What's the big deal? You do the crime, you do the time. What's there to be afraid of? Be smart and you can even make it fun.

My only regret was that Jake wasn't up there enough. Sometimes I tried to frame him and get him banished with me, but it never seemed to work. He lives his life in the lines, like he colors. Hates trouble. I asked him a thousand times. I'm asking now: What are you so scared of?

Oh, another regret. I don't get sent to the Cool-It Room anymore. Dad says I've outgrown it. Now I get "big girl" punishments, like grounding and cutting my allowance.

Jake

I am *not* scared. I just don't get into trouble, that's all. Why should I? Trouble means punishment. Who needs that? I'd have to be loony. And I'm not loony. I'm sensible. Even my mother says it. "My sensible boy," she calls me sometimes. "My spunky girl," she calls Lily. "Cool," says Lily. "I'd rather have spunk than sense." I rest my case.

Anyway, when Lily came down from the Cool-It Room on the day of the big sombrero choke-off, she said to Mom and Dad, "That was a lie what Bump said, wasn't it? Me and Jake are really twins, right? Even if we look different?" I thought her voice sounded wobbly, and when I looked I saw she was ready to cry. Mom grabbed her. "Of course you are, honey. You know why?" "Why?" sobbed

Lily. "Because you were both twin eggs inside Mommy at the same time. So there." Suddenly Lily was beaming and dancing and shaking her fist at Bump, wherever he was: "Yeah! Twin eggs!"

But all that got me thinking. That night in our bunks I said up to Lily, "So I guess we can be twins and still be different."

"Duh," said Lily. "In case you didn't notice, you're a boy and I'm a girl."

"I mean different in other stuff," I said.

"What other stuff?"

"I don't know, like, almost everything."

She threw her stuffed pig at me. "That's a lie. We're not different in everything."

I ticked off a few things. "You get in trouble. I don't. You can't stay still. I can. You collect train stuff. I collect stones. You hate dogs. I hate worms. You like chocolate. I like strawberry—"

"We *both* like pumpkin seeds," she butted in.

"Yeah," I said, "but I don't steal yours."

She crowed, "And we *both* have goombla! What about *that*?"

"Big deal," I said. "That's the only thing. Everything else is different."

"We are *not* different."

"Yes we are."

"Bull," she said, and down came her stuffed watermelon.

"See?" I said. "Who else sleeps with a water-melon?"

That bunk-time argument went on for months. Every time we did something different, I said, "See?" Every time we did something the same, she said, "See?" But most of the things we did the same were because she made it happen that way, so she would be right about us not being different. Like one day we got ice-cream cones and she got strawberry.

"I know why you're doing that," I said.

"Doing what?" she said, as if she didn't know.

"Eating strawberry. So we'll be the same."

"I can eat strawberry if I want."

"You never ate strawberry in your life. You hate strawberry."

"I *love* strawberry," she screeched. "I hate *you*." She knocked my ice-cream cone to the ground.

"See how different we are," I said, all calm. "I would never do that."

Lily kept trying to cram us into sameness, but

the differences kept popping out.

When we were nine we played Pee Wee Baseball. Our team was the Robins. Lily was a pitcher. I was a catcher. One day we played the Beagles, and Lily was pitching against Bump Stubbins. Bump whiffed at three straight pitches, but when the umpire called, "Strike three!" Bump just stayed there, digging into the batter's box. "Strike three," the ump said again, and Bump looks up to him and says, "It's only two strikes." "It's three, son," says the ump, and Bump goes bananas. His Mohawk is gone by now but his personality is even worse. He starts pounding the plate with his bat and screaming, "Strike two! Strike two!" He slams his cap to the ground. He's red in the face. He wails like a baby. It's one of the all-time tantrums. I have a front-row seat. I take off my catcher's mask so I can see better. Finally the umpire says, "Son, take a seat on the bench. This game is over for you." Kids don't usually get ejected from Pee Wee games, but that's what happened. When Bump didn't go, the ump put some bite in his voice: "Son—go. Now." That sent Bump packing, but it wasn't good enough for Lily. She comes stomping off the mound jabbing her finger at Bump: "Yeah—yer *outta* here! Back to the bench, ya dumb meatball!" And now the ump points to Lily and goes, "And you too, miss. Your game is over." As Lily steamed off to the bench, I actually fell on my back, I was laughing so hard.

In our bunks that night I said, "See? Different. You were pitching. I was catching. You hate Bump. I don't. You were mad. I was laughing. You got thrown out. I didn't."

She got quiet. She said, like to herself, "I was mad. He was laughing." She perked up. "Aha! Mad. Laughing. They're *both* feelings. See—we're the same."

"Get real," I snickered. "Laughing ain't feelings." And I added, just because I felt like it, "Boys don't have feelings."

Lily wouldn't let it go. At dinner the next day she said, "Daddy, Jake keeps saying we're different. Tell him we're not."

Dad put out his hands. "Hey, don't get me in the middle. You guys sort it out."

"You're just exploring your twinness, is all," said Mom. "Argue away."

"But Mom," Lily squealed, "he says boys don't have feelings. They do too, don't they? Tell him."

Mom kept a straight face but her eyes were laughing. "Of course boys have feelings. Sometimes they're just afraid to show it. Boys are funny that way. Your brother loves you. Love is a feeling. Therefore—pass the salt, please—your brother has feelings."

Lily stuck her tongue out at me. "See? You have feelings. You love me."

I didn't say anything.

Lily

That was such bulldung, Jake saying he had no feelings. Even though Mom said I was right, I wanted to prove it for myself. But I was having a hard time.

I made myself cry. I walked up to him with my face full of tears and he said, "What's the matter?"

"My watermelon!" I bawled. "It's lost. I can't find it!"

He shrugged. "It'll show up." He walked away.

Another time I pretended I hurt my knee. I fell to the floor. "Owww!" I screamed.

Jake came running. "What's wrong?"

"I smashed my knee!" I rolled onto my back. "It hurts!"

He helped me to the sofa. He looked at it. "I

don't see no bump or bruise or nothing."

"It hurrrrrts!"

He rubbed it a little. "Don't be a baby. Walk it off." He went away.

Another time I got the story of Babar the elephant. Even now it makes me cry. I took it to Jake. I showed him the saddest page of all, the one where the hunter shoots Babar's mother. Jake looked at the picture. He looked at me. "So?" he said, and walked away.

It was hopeless. I couldn't make him cry. Maybe he was right.

Then I thought of something. Actually, two somethings.

"Mom," I said, "is mad a feeling?"

"Sure," she said. "There are lots of feelings."

"How about scared?" I said. "Is that a feeling too?"

"Absolutely."

Ha—I had him. He had feelings twice. And they happened the two times Mr. No Trouble got in trouble.

Jake

I don't believe you're going to bring that stuff up.

Lily

Watch me.

Trouble & Feeling #1: mad. Jake got in trouble in third grade. The teacher, Miss Ottinger, got fed up with our messy cubbies—except Jake's, of course, which was always perfect. So she told us to straighten them up and she would inspect them. Anybody with a messy cubby would get a detention. So we all cleaned up our cubbies—except for Jake, because he didn't need to—and Miss Ottinger inspected them. Imagine our shock when she told us that everybody's cubby was neat except for one—Jake's!

To this day nobody knows how it happened. Maybe somebody was mad at Jake and messed up his cubby. Whatever, Jake blew a fuse. "That's a lie!" he shouted. "My cubby is neat!"

I don't know what was more shocking, that Jake had a messy cubby or that he blew a fuse. The teacher's eyes boggled. Jake was her little angel. "I'm sorry, Jake," she said (and she looked it), "but fair is fair. You know what I said. You'll stay after school today."

Jake screamed, "No! No! I'm being framed! I didn't do it!"

I already knew some things that Jake couldn't stand, like strawberry ice cream and mushrooms and me putting my finger in his ear. But now I was finding out the thing he hated most of all: getting accused of something he didn't do. For the rest of the afternoon he sat there wagging his head and mumbling, "I didn't do it . . . I didn't do it. . . ."

Late bus for Jake. When the bell rang and everybody else got up to go home, Jake stayed put. So did I. I didn't have any big reason or anything. I just did it. I guess I figured if Jake got detention, so did I. We would both get the late bus.

Jake looked over and growled, "What're you doing here?"

"I'm waiting with you," I said.

"You don't have detention. I do."

"I know," I said.

He practically shoved me off my seat. "So go!" He was screaming again. "It's not you! It's me! I don't want you here!"

I ran from the class. I didn't even get my coat from the cubby. My face was burning.

Trouble & Feeling #2: scared. Jake broke something. One of those tulip-shaped wineglasses. He was snooping in the cupboard where Mom keeps the good dishes and stuff. He decided it would be cool and grown-up to drink water out of a wineglass. So he did. "You better wash it and dry it and put it back so Mom won't know," I warned him. He was washing it when it fell in the sink and broke. Jake went into shock. A funny, squeaky sound was coming out of him.

"Clean it up," I said, "and just don't say anything." For once Jake obeyed me. He knew that when it came to dealing with trouble, I was the expert.

He cleaned it up and that was that—for a while. And then one day at dinner Mom said, "I'm missing a wineglass. Do either of you know about it?"

I've heard of people freezing with fright. That's what Jake did. He froze. He stared at his mashed potatoes. I'm pretty sure Mom noticed and figured it out, but right then I piped up: "I did it."

Why? Who knows? Maybe just out of habit. Maybe I confessed because I took pity on Jake. I knew how he hated getting in trouble.

Or maybe I was just being selfish. Maybe I didn't want to pass up a chance to get sent to the Cool-It Room and work on my burping.

Anyway, they were Jake's two big troubles: The Detention and The Broken Wineglass. So one day I reminded him about them. Of course he denied everything. He said he never got mad about the unfair detention and was never scared about breaking the glass. And anyway, he said, even *if* it was true, it just shows how different we are, because I would not have blown a fuse if I had gotten a detention. And about the broken glass, he said he let me take the punishment because "I knew you love the Cool-It Room so much."

And so the silly argument went on and on—

"We're different."

"No we're not!"

I emailed Poppy from our family computer: "Jake says we're different. He says we're different about everything except we came from twin eggs. Tell him he's wrong, Poppy!!!!!"

Poppy BlackBerried back: "Cool it. It's just a phase. He'll get over it."

Everybody was telling me to cool it. How was I supposed to cool it when I had an aggravating moronic brother?

"We're different."

"No we're not!"

On and on . . .

until . . .

One Day at the Beach. . . .

Jake

We were on vacation in Ocean City. Mom and Dad let us go down to wade, but we weren't allowed to go in deeper than our knees. "If there's an undertow it can sweep you out to sea before you know it," said Dad.

The water was cold at first, but then it felt warm. The surf flopped at our legs. We splashed each other and splashed strangers and ran through the water. Kids were screaming. Seagulls were screaming. Even the sun seemed to be screaming.

When I was finally ready to go back to the blanket, I looked around for Lily. She wasn't there. I came out of the water and stood on the smooth, wet sand. I saw zillions of people, but no Lily. I called, but her name got swallowed up in the noise. I looked out at the endless ocean. I didn't see anybody getting swept out to sea.

I figured she went back to the blanket. I headed onto the dry, soft sand. There were blankets and umbrellas everywhere, but not ours. So I started wandering, looking. And after a while I just wandered. I liked walking through all those people, everybody having fun and laughing and running and shrieking. I knew Lily hadn't found the blanket either. I *knew*. She was out there just like me, wandering, enjoying it all. We were doing it together. I mean, I couldn't reach out and touch her and I couldn't see her. But I knew we were together. She was with me.

So I walked up and down the beach, watching the people. I came to a little kid who was crying. He was lost. I took him to the lifeguard.

I never did find Mom and Dad, but they must have found Lily because I heard her yell, "There he is!" and they were running and screaming, "Jake! Jake!" Then they were hugging the breath out of me and Mom was crying. But not for long. She shook me by the shoulders. She shook Lily.

"What's the matter with you two? You had us worried sick!"

"We were okay, Mom," I said.

She wasn't listening. "You *never* go off wandering like that again! How did we know the undertow didn't get you?"

"Mom, we did just like you said. We only went in up to our knees."

"Why didn't you go to the lifeguard? You know you're supposed to go to the lifeguard if you're lost!"

It was hard to look up at her because of the sun. I had to close my eyes. "Mom," I said, "cool it. We weren't lost."

Lily poked Mom. "See? That's what I told you."

I think that's the closest we ever came to telling our parents about goombla. But even if we wanted to, what would we say? *Mom. Dad. We weren't lost because we were with each other. We can be with each other even when we can't see each other. Even if we're miles apart.*

Who's going to believe that, or understand it?

So I just said, "Mom, we're *okay*. We'll go to the lifeguard next time. Promise."

Lily was grinning. I looked at her hand. Her fingers were crossed.

I have to admit it was pretty neato. I forgot all about being different.

Lily

When we got home from vacation, we talked about it in our bunks that night.

"Were you ever lost at the beach today?"

"No. You?"

"No."

"Ever *feel* lost?"

"No."

Hey, we weren't stupid. We knew what the word *lost* meant, at least if it had to do with something we owned. I lost my flip-flop. I lost my dollar. But we didn't really know what it meant when it came to ourselves. We always felt as if we were together. As I was wandering around the beach that day, in and out of all those people and blankets, it felt as if Jake was walking right beside me. As if he was poking me in the ribs and saying, "Look at that! . . . Look at *that*!"

I guess it had been that way all our life, but the beach day brought it to our attention. And suddenly we had this cool new goombla thing to share, like birthday nights at the train station. We were . . . The Neverlost Twins. So I didn't hear any more of that slop about how different we were for a while.

And then, by fall, I started to hear the D-word again.

"We're different."

"No we're not."

Until The Great Snow-Fort War.

Jake

It was the first big snow of the year. We had a snow day from school. Lily and I decided to make a snow fort. We went up the street to the vacant lot where we often played. Of course, first we had to have a snowball fight. Then we thought, *Let's make two forts and we can bomb each other.* So that's what we did.

Just when I finished my fort, I had to run back home to go to the bathroom. I was in the bathroom when I felt something on my arm. I rolled up my sleeve. There was a bruise. I touched it. It hurt. But that wasn't all. When I touched the bruise, it was like pressing a button. It spoke to me, one word. *Lily!* When I say it spoke to me, I don't mean in the usual way. I didn't hear the word. I felt it.

But I felt that word as loud and clear as I had ever heard a word. And somehow just that—*Lily!*—told me she was in trouble.

I didn't even roll down my sleeve or put my winter coat back on. I raced down the stairs and up the street. Before I got there I heard the screams. But they weren't Lily's. Then what I saw were two things: the roof of Lily's fort was caved in, and Lily was sitting on top of somebody, mashing the kid's face into the snow. The kid was screaming and flailing his arms and Lily was mashing away and riding the body like a bucking bronco. I didn't have to be a genius to figure out the kid had to be Bump Stubbins.

So Bump finally manages to flail and scream his way loose, and he runs off a ways and turns and wipes his snowy face and splutters at Lily, "You'll pay for this! Yer dead meat! Yer lucky I don't hit girls. Yer lucky yer brother showed up! Yer luck—" Lily took a step toward him and he hightailed it outta there.

Lily had to stop laughing to tell me about it. She was inside her fort when suddenly she heard somebody yell, "Geronimo!" and the roof came crashing in on her, followed by Bump Stubbins. Bump seemed surprised to find somebody inside the fort he had just body-bombed, but he didn't seem especially bothered. In fact, when he saw it was Lily, he smirked and said, "That's for choking me."

Big mistake.

Before Bump knew what happened, Lily was scrubbing the snow, and his face was the mop.

When we finished laughing, we squeezed into my fort for a while, but that was boring. So we had another snowball fight and headed home. Along the way I remembered my arm. I told her what happened in the bathroom, how I felt something and touched the bruise and sort of heard her name. "See," I said. I showed her my arm. I boggled—the bruise was gone. She looked at me, like, *Yeah, right.* And then her eyes got wide at me. She yanked off her coat and rolled up her sleeve and there it was— same bruise, same spot—only now it was on *her* arm. She wonder-said, "That's where he landed on me."

We rolled down our sleeves and stared at each other and walked on.

"Look," she said as we came to our porch. A pair of sandals was sitting by the front door. Sandals? In the snow?

"Who's here?" I said.

We went inside. Lily saw him first. She screamed: "Poppy!"

Lily

I jumped into him so hard he went, "Ouff!" and fell back on the sofa. We swarmed over him, first with ourselves, then with questions.

"Poppy! Aren't your feet cold?"

"Poppy! Did you find yourself?"

"Poppy! How long are you staying?"

I think the answers were "Freezing," "Yep," and "Till you kick me out."

Poppy's hair was still long but now it was white and tied in a ponytail. Dad brought him a pair of socks for his bare feet. "I guess I've been to too many warm places lately," he said. "I forgot about snow."

We talked and talked till my tongue got tired. We had pizza and chicken wings delivered, and we could hardly eat we were talking so much. Relatives came over and we ordered more pizza and wings. Jake and I put on our sombreros and said *si* instead of yes whenever we got a chance.

When the visitors left, Poppy reached behind the sofa and pulled out a little green sack. There were two things in it, identical as usual. "They're castanets," he said. They reminded me of clamshells. He showed us how to hold them and make them clack. "Now you can sing and dance too."

Poppy slept in the spare room. We sat on his blankets in our pj's till after midnight. Mom had to kick us out.

We prayed for another snow day but when morning came, no luck. Poppy wanted to sleep in but we wouldn't let him. We dragged him down to breakfast. Mom made waffles, a dead giveaway that these were special times.

Poppy walked us to school. He wore Dad's socks under his sandals. We wanted him to come in. "You can talk about geography!" I said. "They'll bring you a grown-up-sized chair," Jake said. He laughed and said no thanks. He was waiting for us when school got out.

Poppy hates malls so we stayed away from them. In fact we didn't go places much at all. He just wanted to stay home and play Monopoly and poker, and talk. "Good grief," Mom said to me and Jake on the second night, "don't you two ever run out of questions? Give your poor Poppy a break."

"Poppy, did you ever get attacked by pirates?" (No.)

"Poppy, did you ever eat eels?" (Yes. And snakes and grasshoppers.)

"Poppy, were you a hippie?" (Definitely.)

After lights-out the second night I asked Jake if he thought it was okay to ask Poppy about Grandma. Up until then we were afraid to, like it was taboo. But I was getting itchy.

"No," said Jake flat out.

"Why not?" I said.

"Because," he said.

"That's not a reason," I said.

"Go to sleep," he said.

So next night at dinner I said, "Poppy, was Grandma a hippie too?"

Mom and Dad stopped chewing. Jake glared at me. The only one who didn't seem bothered was Poppy. Not just his mouth but his whole face smiled, and he said, "I thought you'd never ask." And we were off to the races.

"Let's see . . . ," he said. "Grandma danced on the beach and she did sit-ins for civil rights and she marched against the war and she said stuff like 'Far out' and 'Groovy' and she wore bell-bottom pants and she drank carrot juice and her feet were always dirty . . . so . . . yeah, Grandma was a hippie too, just like me. In fact, now that I think about it, that's pretty much how hippies came—in pairs."

We didn't have to ask more questions. Poppy just went on and on about his life with Grandma in California. They had lots of jobs, from waiting on tables to picking oranges. They were living over a garage when Mom was born. Mom laughed: "I was a hippie baby!" They named her Dovey, as a sign of peace.

It must have been a nice garage, because a year later they had another baby, Uncle Peaceboy. They lived over the garage till the kids were in high school. Poppy and Grandma got regular jobs and started to look more like regular people. They started wearing shoes and they didn't dance on the beach much anymore. "One thing I wouldn't give up," said Poppy, "my long hair." He laughed. "Barbers hated me."

When Mom and Uncle Peaceboy grew up and moved away, Grandma and Poppy junked all their shoes but their sandals. Poppy burned his one necktie and they went back to being big-time hippies. "Except nobody called us that anymore," said Poppy, looking a little sad. "The war was over and so was the age of the hippies. We sort of discovered the earth. Everything from fish to snails was in danger. The air stank and the water was disappearing. I think we might have been the first of the greenies. That's when your grandma started climbing trees."

Jake

In the dark that night Lily hung upside down from her top bunk. "We gotta tell Poppy."

I knew what she was talking about, but I pretended I didn't. "Tell him what?"

"You know. About us. *Us*. Goombla."

"It's a secret," I said. "We don't even tell our parents."

"Poppy's different. You can tell a grandparent anything."

"I don't think so," I said. "Go to sleep."

She punched me in the arm. "I'm telling him. I *have* to. I have to tell *somebody*."

I wasn't surprised. Besides cheating and lying and confessing, she's also the world's worst secret keeper. "You better not," I said, and went to sleep.

What I didn't say was that I actually didn't care that much. In fact, I had kind of been wanting to tell somebody too.

But we weren't the only ones with something to tell. Poppy surprised us in the morning. He was at the kitchen table with our parents when we came down for breakfast.

"What are you doing here?" Lily asked him.

"Eating an English muffin with jelly," he said. I guess you could say that was the truth but not the whole truth.

Mom and Dad grabbed their tool belts and headed out the door for work. And Poppy dropped the bomb. He told us he was leaving next day.

Lily squawked, "You said you're staying till we kick you out!"

"I know," he said. "I guess I lied."

Lily threw an English muffin at him. "I don't like you, Poppy."

She didn't stop grumping until Poppy hauled her onto his lap and made her laugh with funny faces. He told us that because he was leaving next day, Mom and Dad said we could stay home from school. And that's when we told him. We told him about the first sleepwalk to the train station and all the birthday-night sleepwalks since then. We told him about the day at the beach and Neverlost, and about The Great Snow-Fort War and The Bruise That Moved.

We told him about the time Lily yelled, "I'm stuck!" only it was me who was stuck in the backyard. And the time I yelled, "Stop!" when Lily was ready to chase a ball into the street five miles away.

We told him—well, Lily told him—her idea that "the rest of us" was born during that first sleepwalk to the station. We told him we know who we are now, but we can't put it into words. We know we have a special thing, we told him, but we can't even describe it to ourselves, so we call it goombla.

Poppy nodded and smiled. The only thing he said was, "Wow," now and then. By the time we were done telling him, it was almost lunchtime. The breakfast dishes were still on the table and we hadn't brushed our teeth.

We told Poppy he was the only one who knew besides us. We made him promise not to tell Mom and Dad. We asked him what he thought about all the stuff we told him. He grinned. "Well, as your grandma would have said a long time ago: *far out*."

Poppy had recently gotten his driver's license in California, so that night he borrowed Dad's car and drove Lily and me to French Creek State Park. He didn't tell us why. He did tell us there were two places where he finally found himself, and he was driving us to one of them. "French Creek State Park is where you found yourself?" I said. "Well, not exactly," he said, and refused to say any more. This drove Lily crazy, of course, because besides being a cheater, liar, confessor, secret-spiller, and pumpkin seed–stealer, she can't stand waiting. She bugged him all the way: Poppy this and Poppy that, until he growled, "Lily, zip it." She did. Poppy is the only person who can make her shut up.

When we got there, Poppy drove through a parking lot and past some log cabins and down a skinny, winding road. He pulled off to the side, onto the grass. "Wait here a sec," he said. He got out, looked at the sky, came back. "I think we're good. Clear but no moon. Let's go."

It was really dark. No streetlights here. Poppy

took each of us by the hand. It seemed like we were walking onto a big flat field. Snow crunched under our boots.

After a while we stopped. Poppy said, "This looks good. Time to lie down, kiddos." He made us lie down with him in the snow, one on either side. "Okay," he said, "all you need to do now is open your eyes and let the universe pour in." While we looked at the stars, Poppy started talking. His voice didn't need to be loud. It was the only sound in the night.

"I was in Chile," he said. "I hired onto a boat bringing fruit up to the US, but it wasn't leaving for a week. So I rented a car and drove out to the Atacama. The Atacama is a desert in northern Chile. It's the driest place on earth. Sometimes they find mummified people and animals there. It's a natural mummy maker." That made us laugh. We didn't laugh again. From then on it was some of the fiercest listening I ever did.

"When I got there, I think maybe I finally felt like I was where I belonged. Like, without Grandma, my life was a match for the Atacama. Ha! Together at last, the two driest deserts in the world.

"So I got out of the car and just started walking. The sun was setting and next thing I knew it was night. I don't know how long I walked with my eyes to the dry, parched earth. Ha." He kind of laughed, but we both knew it wasn't a laughy laugh so we didn't join in. "Yeah, I guess I do know— about ten years. Anyway, I don't know what it was. Maybe when you're completely dry and empty, up is the only way to look. So I looked up.

"And I wish I could tell you how I felt. That's why I understand when you say you can't explain your special thing, your goombla. I looked up and for the first time in my life I wasn't just looking—I was *seeing*. Suddenly the word *sky* seemed so flimsy. Useless. For one thing, I had never known there were so many stars up there. There's no light pollution from cities out there in the Atacama, and just like tonight, no moon to wash out the starlight.

"But that was only the beginning, the wonder of that blizzard of stars. Something else was happening. With Grandma, my world was the earth. The earth of trees and oceans and people and sockeye salmon. Now the night in the Atacama

seemed to be telling me something: look . . .
look . . . there is *more.* I saw a gusher of stars from
one end to the other and I thought, *It's the Milky
Way! My galaxy!* I was filled with a sense that
I belonged to something way bigger than I ever
imagined. Than I ever *could* imagine. The ends of
it were unreachable. I could travel at light speed
for a million lifetimes and I would barely get out
of the driveway.

"But you know what got to me most?" We
were both too mesmerized to ask. "It wasn't the
sense of the vast endlessness of it all. It was just
the opposite. It wasn't that it was all too much
for me to comprehend. It was that no matter how
big and unimaginable it was, it was my home.
My ultimate neighborhood. My hometown. It was
where I belonged. And—here was the best part—
so did everybody else belong. Everybody who is
and everybody who ever was. I wasn't alone after
all. I was connected to it all. That star there"—he
pointed—"it's my neighbor . . . and that one . . .
and that one. . . . And Grandma. For the first time
in ten years I sensed her presence in something
that wasn't a picture or a memory. She was out

there too—but not really *there*, because everything is *here*. And that's where"—he took my hand, and I knew on the other side he was taking Lily's—"that's where I found myself. There." He brought our hands to his heart. *"Here."*

Lily

Even before Poppy said Grandma was out there, I knew he was talking about more than stars. When Poppy stopped talking, we just lay there in the snow, looking up. After a while I started to feel what Poppy felt. I started to feel comfortable, at home, like the world was our room, like the stars were our ceiling.

On the ride home Poppy told us about entanglement. He said entanglement shows that everything in the universe is connected. He said that light is made up of particles called photons. "Sometimes," he said, "photons come in pairs. It's called entanglement." He looked at us squeezed into the shotgun seat. "You could call them twins." I jabbed Jake in the ribs. Poppy said if twin photons are separated, they still act as if they're together. You could put them on opposite ends of the universe and it wouldn't make any difference. "If you tweak one photon," he said, "the twin on the other side of the universe will twitch."

I jabbed Jake again, hard this time. *"See?"*

Jake squawked. "Ow!"

I was so busy thinking about entangled twin light particles that we were on the porch at home before I remembered something. "Poppy!" I said. "You said you found yourself in two places. Where's the other one?"

He didn't say a word. He took a step back. His grin got bigger and bigger under the porch light. When it seemed his grin was ready to crack his face in half, he pointed with both index fingers— straight at us. And grabbed us in a bear hug that lasted forever.

THE END

Jake

I knew she would try to end it there. She says that since I had the first chapter, she gets the last and so she gets to end it wherever she wants. But somebody's gotta be the Whole Story Police here, and the hug on the porch *wasn't* the end.

In the first place, the bear hug didn't last forever. It lasted about five minutes—which, I admit, is pretty darn long for a hug. Even the hug when Poppy left next day wasn't as long. Lily was mad and thumping his chest one minute, bawling into his arms the next. Poppy said don't worry, it wouldn't be another ten years before he showed up again. I'm not sure we believed him.

Before Dad drove us all to the airport, Poppy came into our room and got all whispery. "Listen," he said, "I have a suggestion for you two. Okay?" We said okay. "So here's what I'd like you to do. I'd like you to write down your story. The story of you two. Your goombla. Like you told me yesterday. I wish I had done it when I was your age. I can hardly remember those days now. I know it's hard to put into words, like you said, but I want you to at least try to write your story down before you become an old poop like me who can't remember anything." Then he pulled two notebooks from the bag he was holding. He gave each of us a pen. "Okay?"

"Okay," we said together.

So we took Poppy to the airport and hugged some more and waved good-bye. We wouldn't leave the terminal until we saw his plane take off and disappear into the clouds.

That night after dinner we started writing in our notebooks. And today, just this second, we finished our book. And that's what you just read.

Okay, say it now. . . .

Lily

THE END

oops

Intro II

Okay, so we made a mistake. Hey, we never wrote a book before.

You're always in such a hurry to get to the end.

I am not.

You read the last page of books first.

I skim. Anyway, for this second intro, I (Lily) wrote that first line up there.

She confessed.

For both of us.

I'm still older than you.

Ignore him. So we figured the book was done last November.

Poppy was gone.

Nothing much happened for a long time.

Except school.

Whoopee.

And then suddenly on a dark and stormy night

Oh, good grief. It was yesterday at dinner.

I was just trying to be literary, since we're back to writing a book.

From now on it's going to be more like a journal. Or a diary. Day-to-day.

Whatever. So *yesterday* at dinner Dad says

Mom says.

Right. Mom says, "So what're you guys gonna do this summer?"

She said it because the school year was over next day.

Right. And we just looked at each other for five seconds

ten seconds

and we both said the word at once:

"Write."

This was no big deal to Mom and Dad.

Just another twins thing.

They asked us what we're going to write.

We just said, "Oh, whatever."

After dinner we went to CVS. I got a new notebook.

I got a new notebook.

So, what's your first line going to be?

Don't know. My head's a blank.

So what's new?

Ha-ha.

How about "Once upon a time . . ."

Right.

Or "It was a dark and stormy night. . . ."

If you don't shut up, I'm never going to start.

Ladies and gentlemen, my sister . . .

Lily

School's out! EEYYESSSSSSS!!!!!!!

Poppy said we don't have to write in our journals every day about every little thing. Just stuff that seems important or interesting. Well—helloooo?—what's more important than summer vacation? I counted on the calendar. We don't go back to school for—*ta-da*—81 days. Eight. Tee. One. In other words—forever! Our fifth-grade teacher, Mrs. Webber, said, "Now, young people, don't waste your summer. Read. Volunteer. Improve yourselves. Be productive." Yeah, I'll be productive all right. I'll tell you what I'm gonna produce. I'm gonna produce fun. Fun! Fun! Fun!

Jake

Don't tell my sister, but forever is already down to 75 days. I'm just starting my notebook because I've been busy getting my new room ready. On the second day of forever Dad made an announcement at dinner: "Good news, guys. You're each going to have your own room."

I pumped my fists. "Yes!"

Lily snickered. "That'll be the day."

Dad rolled on. "You'll stay where you are, Lily girl. You'll get a regular bed now. The bunks will go." He nodded to me. "You'll get the room next to hers."

Lily wasn't snickering now. She was squawking. "He can't move there! That's Poppy's room!"

"We'll fix up the attic for Poppy," said Dad.

Lily snapped away from him. "Mom—he *can't*! Tell him!"

Mom gave a big, sad sigh. She patted Lily's hand. "It's time, honey."

Lily snatched her hand away. "Don't touch me." She swung back to Dad. She put on her sob face. "But Dad, you *can't* separate us. We're *twins*."

"You're also boy and girl," Dad reminded her. "You're not little kids anymore. You need your own rooms. Stop acting like it's the end of the world. He's not moving to Timbuktu. He's moving a couple feet down the hall. You can visit each other all you want."

Amazingly, my sister didn't say another word. She just stared bug-eyed off into space. She was in shock. Then she dropped her fork to the floor and left the table.

So next day we moved—Dad and I, that is. Lily sat in the doorway and made us step over her the whole time.

That was four days ago. For four days Lily glared and grumped and slumped. Then yesterday morning she barges into my new room and shakes me awake and says, "Let's ride."

So we rode our bikes.

And we went to the creek to hunt stones for my collection.

We went to the comic shop.

And we went to Little Train That Could, the model railroad shop, so Lily could stare at an American Flyer blue-and-silver diesel engine that she says is just like the California Zephyr dream train that streaks through us once a year on our birthday night.

And we checked in with Mom and Dad twice at the house they're working on down the street. Nobody is living in it. It's what builders call a handyman special. That means it's cheap because it needs a lot of fixing, which is where Mom and Dad come in. Because it's so close and because we check in, we're allowed to stay at our house by ourselves this summer.

And we tried to play hide-and-seek, but we still can't because we always know where the other is hiding.

And Lily tried to teach me to burp on command.

That's what we were doing when a funny thing happened.

Lily

There was nothing funny about it. As I was demonstrating a simple beginner's burp, the doorbell rang. We ran for it but nobody was there. But something was. On the doormat. A stone. A blue stone. Jake of course was impressed. "Blue," he said. "Cool." He took it to our—ex-*cuse* me, *his*—room and put it in the new box Mom made for his collection.

Me, I just had a bad feeling. I tried to be happy for him. I know how much he loves cool stones. But the bad feeling stuck. And got badder, because in the next couple days two more stones showed up: a pink one and a gold one.

I told him, "That's not real gold. It's fool's gold. It's fake."

He shrugged. "I know."

I told him, "These don't count. They're stuff you buy at a hobby place or a museum. You should just have stones you find yourself. That's a *real* collection."

He didn't even hear me. He just ran upstairs pumping his fist: "Yes!"

No stone came yesterday, but my bad feeling got a name. Jake and I were out riding our bikes when we ran into Bump Stubbins and his gang. Not long ago Bump dug up two other nitwits from under a rotting log, and now the three of them ride around together and call themselves the Death Rays. As we were cruising past them, Bump called out, "Hey, Jake! D'juh like the stones?"

Jake shot a look at Bump, all surprised. It had never occurred to him this was where the stones came from. My brother can be a real moron sometimes. I picked up speed. "C'mon," I said.

I thought Jake was going to do it right, but when we were half a block past them he looked back and called, "Yeah! Thanks!"

Last night I got out the cards to play poker, but Jake didn't want to. Not even when I promised I wouldn't cheat. He just kept making goo-goo eyes at the new stones. He's already making plans for a bigger collection box. "How many more do you think I'll get?" he said. "As many as it takes to make you kiss him," I said. His face got all frowny. He just didn't get it.

"Jake," I said, "why do you think he's giving you stones? Because he's trying to suck up to you. He hates me because I beat him up and struck him out, so he's trying to take you away."

"Away from what?" he said.

"Away from *me*, dumbo."

He just laughed and ran downstairs to check the doormat.

Today we were out riding again, and again we ran into the Bumpsters. Bump called, "Hey, Jake! C'mon and ride with the Death Rays!"

Jake gave a little wave and said, "Nah." *Right answer*, I thought, feeling great. But then he said something that gave me the chills: "Not today."

Like, not today—but maybe tomorrow?

Jake

I don't know why my sister is getting all dramatic. What's the big deal? If somebody wants to give me cool stones, why shouldn't I take them? What am I supposed to do, say, "Here, take 'em back. I don't want 'em"? How stupid is that? I mean, if Bump Stubbins left an American Flyer California Zephyr engine on the doormat for her, what do you think she would do—throw it in the trash? Yeah, right.

Okay, she hates him. I get it. I don't even blame her. But what's he ever done to *me*? Am I supposed to hate everybody my sister hates? Are my sister's enemies my enemies? Is that what being twins is all about? Lily sees all this evil stuff in Bump. I just see a clown. He's harmless. He's just a kid, that's all. A guy. That's what all three of them are, just guys out riding around. So why shouldn't I ride with them?

Lily

I could see it coming. I could see his goo-goo eyes every time we saw the Bumpsters riding around. I figured sooner or later he would join them. Just thinking about it made me mad. Mad enough to decide that when it finally happened, I would just spit, burp, and call, "Good riddance! Who needs ya? Who cares?"

So when I saw that his bike was gone one day, I reminded myself, *Who cares?* I went out riding myself. Why not? I'm a big girl. I pedaled past Mom and Dad working on the handyman special. When I saw the Bumpsters riding up ahead of me I said to myself, *Turn off. Go another way.* But my bike didn't listen. It just kept following them. And then they saw me, and that's when they made their big mistake—they sped up. All my reminders went out the window. Were they serious? Did they really think they could outrace me? *Me?*

I took off after them. They zipped down street after street. Hills. Alleys. Parking lots. Leaning into turns like motorcycle riders. I would have caught them sooner but I couldn't stop laughing at those four Bumpster hineys slamming from side to side. I caught them on the flat stretch of Beacon Street that runs along the tracks.

I don't know what they expected me to do. Heck, I don't even know what *I* expected. But as soon as I pulled up to their fenders I knew: I had already done it. Caught up. All I had to do now was beat them. I smoked past them like they were standing still. I was laughing and waving. Turns out I didn't feel mad or bad at all. I felt great!

(And just to set the record straight—*if* a train left on the doormat came from BS, yeah, I *would* throw it in the trash.)

Jake

I'm happy for you. I'm glad you felt so great. But let me tell you something you don't know, since all you want to do is tell everybody what a bad brother I am these days. When you went past us laughing and flapping your arms and shrieking, "Beatcha, Bumpsters!" I had a little grin on my face. I was kinda proud, like, *Death Rays, meet my sister.* You didn't catch that, did you?

Lily

No, I sure didn't. Must have been the littlest grin of all time. What good was it if nobody saw it? And what did you *say*? Huh? *Death Rays, meet my sister.* Did you say it out loud? Huh? Go ahead, tell the readers. Tell them how you opened your mouth and shouted it to the world and stuck up for me. Tell them how you went to war for your sister. Go ahead. Do it now. I'll give you the next page to answer. . . .

Jake

Lily

No answer? Didn't think so.

So today he goes out riding with his bumpy boys again, and sure enough I run into them pedaling their bumpy butts down by the park. I'm ready to smoke them again but a funny thing happens—they don't speed up. They just go cruising along like I'm not there.

I called, "Hey Jake! I'm going to the comic shop. Wanna come?"

He called back, "Later."

"Where're you going?" I called.

"Nowhere."

I didn't like his answers. I didn't like the way the summer was going so far. Most of all I didn't like being alone. So I caught up with them. I pedaled alongside. I didn't say anything. I just stared straight ahead, minded my own business. They turned a corner, I turned a corner. Finally they turned into the parking lot of Mike Ivey's Auto Repair. They stopped. I stopped. Nobody said anything. They just glared at me, all but Jake. He stared at the sky, the ground, everywhere but me.

Finally the Big Bumpster spoke up. "What're you doing?"

"What's it look like?" I said.

"You can't come with us."

I sneered. "First of all, genius, I can go anywhere I want. It's a free country. And second of all, I'm not going *anywhere* with you. I'm going with my brother."

"Not now you're not." He was chewing licorice. His teeth were outlined in black, like a cartoon.

I foot-wheeled my bike up to his. "You gonna stop me, snow face?" Up close, I couldn't help noticing he was bigger than he was the day I trashed him at the snow fort.

He got all smuggy. "I don't *have* to stop you. He's with *us*. That's the way it is."

"You think you can buy off my brother with a

couple stones?" I said.

One of the assistant morons butted in. "He's one of us, girlie. He's a Death Ray."

I laughed. "Yeah, right."

The assistant moron shoved his face into mine. He grinned. "Ask him." On the assistant moron's face were more freckles than the French Creek sky has stars. I looked at Jake. I gagged out the words: "Are you a Death Ray?"

He didn't look at me. He didn't speak. He didn't have to. I knew the answer.

They saddled up and rode. I couldn't move. The world was suddenly tilted, like it was trying to dump me off. I guess the world didn't know something—I don't like to get dumped. I went after them.

When I caught up, the Bumpster snarled, "What part of we-don't-want-you don't you understand?"

"I don't care if he's ten Death Rays," I said. "He's my brother first. And I'm his sister. You can't change that, moron."

"Yeah, well, I got news for *you*. You're something else too."

"Oh really."

"Yeah. You're a *girl*." He sneered the last word.

"That so?"

"Yeah, and this is boys only. It's a boys-only gang and we're going to our boys-only hideout. So until you change your sex, girlie"—he spit licorice juice on the ground—"scram."

They took off. Their tires flung gravel on my shoes. "Jake?" I called. "Jake?"

But Jake was riding.

Jake

Did I feel bad? There's Lily calling after me and I'm riding away. Sure I felt bad. I'm not a monster. But here's the thing she doesn't get: it's no big deal. Nothing strange is going on here. Nothing evil. Nothing tragic. The only thing going on here is growing up. When guys get older they start to hang with each other. It's, like, the herd instinct. It's normal. No big deal. She thinks I'm the villain. I'm not the villain. I'm just a kid trying to grow up.

What does she want? Does she want me to spend my whole life with nobody but her? *Oh look, there's Jake and Lily. They're seventy-nine years old and they still play poker and ride bikes together. They still hear each other five miles away. Still sleep in the same bedroom. You can't tear them apart. Aren't they adorable. Twinny-twin twins.*

Personally, I think Lily is starting to lose her marbles. Maybe she's allergic to something in the air and it's making her goofy. When Bump reminded her she's a girl and told her to scram and we rode away, she says she called after me, right? Called my name. That's not the only thing she called. She called, "I'm *not* a girl!"

You believe it?

Lily

No I didn't.

did i?

Jake

Yeah, you did. Tell Mom and Dad to take you to an allergy doctor. Or a shrink.

Anyway, the point is, whatever my sister thinks, we're harmless. We're just four kids who call ourselves the Death Rays. The name is supposed to be funny, but of course she doesn't get it. We don't go around zapping people. We ride bikes and hang in our hideout. It's nothing fancy. It's just a cool tree. You ride down by the tracks and you walk your bikes over the tracks and into the woods between the tracks and the creek. It's somewhere past the stone bridge, but that's all I'm going to say. There's this funny kind of tree—or maybe it's a bush—whatever. The branches don't stick up in the air but they bend and come down to the ground until the whole thing looks kind of like a big leafy umbrella. What you do is, you poke your way through the branches and—presto!—you're inside this kind of dome-shaped natural hut. I mean, it's just begging you to come in and hang out.

So that's what we do. We sit down. We talk. We tell jokes. We compare penknives. If we picked up stuff at a store, we eat: Twinkies, hoagies, sodas. The four of us. Me. Bump. A freckled kid named Nacho. And a tall skinny kid named Burke.

Really evil, huh?

When we're not in the hideout, we're riding around doing stuff.

Like skipping flat stones across the creek.

Like ringing doorbells and running.

Like spit-bombing cars from the Airy Street bridge.

Like picking out someone on the sidewalk downtown and walking really *really* close behind them until they notice us and then we run and laugh our butts off.

But mostly we go goobering.

Goobers. That's Bump's name for somebody that's funny. Funny-different. Funny-weird. A laugh magnet. No—a laugh target. When he spots one he calls out, "Goober!" If Bump were a hunting dog, his nose would stick out and his tail would go straight up.

Of course, we'd been coming across goobers all our lives. We noticed them, but just barely. They maybe registered 0.2 on a scale of 1–10. They weren't important enough to give a name to.

Bump changed all that. He hauled them onto the stage. He threw the spotlight on them. Suddenly they were 10s.

Already this summer we've found some real winners:

- A boy goober wearing big white-framed sunglasses. Probably stole them from his mother and thought they were cool.
- A girl wearing a T-shirt that said BAN BISON BURGERS.
- A girl walking out of the library with a stack of books up to her chin. (We called, "It's summer vacaaaaaa-tion!")
- An old man we see every day who's The Slowest Person On Earth. He shuffles along

with one of those four-legged aluminum walker things. Bump brought a watch one day and we timed him crossing the street. It took him *twenty-eight seconds* curb to curb!

• A lady in a purple sweat suit who doesn't just walk or jog down the street. Instead she skips and dances and doesn't even notice everybody staring at her.

Not all goobers are discovered just haphazard as we ride around. Bump goes out scouting on his own. He'll spot a goober and check its location. All he says next day is, "Follow me." Sometimes we ride clear across town, to neighborhoods we don't even recognize. When he stops, he doesn't have to say anything. There's no "Goober!" call. We just sit there leg-leaning on our bikes, waiting for it to appear.

But what happened today was different from every other goober spotting so far. First thing this morning Bump said, "Let's go to the hideout." He was acting funny. Quiet. Something was on his mind. He just sat on the ground chewing his black licorice. He's always got a wad in his mouth.

When we were all seated in the hideout, nobody said anything. Until I spoke up: "What's wrong, Bump?"

So far Bump's face had been a blank. Now suddenly his mouth cracked into a smirk. "Wrong?" he said. "Ain't nothin' *wrong*. It might be the *rightest* thing ever."

Now he really had our attention. "What're you talking about?" I said.

"I saw something," he said. Now he seemed puzzled. He looked up, as if he was trying to see through the domed leafy roof of the hideout.

"What?" Nacho and Burke said together.

"Where?" I said.

Bump was shaking his head. "I . . . I . . ." He couldn't seem to find words.

I tried to help him out. "You saw a goober?"

He laughed out loud. He wagged his head. "Goober? Goober ain't even good enough."

I poked him. "C'mon, Bump. *What?*"

He brought his eyes down from the leaves. He looked at each of us. He had a dreamy, blinky look, like he had seen a miracle. "Last night . . . after dinner . . . I was just riding. . . ."

"Yeah? Yeah?" we said.

"I saw something. . . . I saw something and I . . . I almost rounded you guys up right then"—he stared at us—"*right then*. But"—he shrugged—"I didn't. I rode home. I almost got run down by a car, I was so . . . so . . ."

"What'd you see, Bump?" said Nacho.

"You gotta tell us," said Burke.

"That's the thing," said Bump. "I'm not even sure. I mean, I *thought* I was sure. Then I went to bed, and when I woke up this morning and the sun was shining through the window and all, I thought, *Nah, couldn't be. Musta been a mirage. A hallu*—"

"Hallucination?" I helped.

"Yeah. I figured it couldna been real."

"So what're you going to do?" said Burke.

Bump took a deep breath. "I'm gonna check it out again. Today. And if it *is* real"—he spit out the licorice wad—"you ain't *never* gonna forget tomorrow."

Lily

Jake looks like he's having the time of his life, and I'm not part of it. Things were great for a while, after we shared the snow-fort bruise. That got him off the we're-different kick. But now it's back, worse than ever.

Some of me is stunned. Shocked. Like I've been walloped by a two-by-four. The rest of me is sad. My heart hurts.

When he's not riding with *them* or in their stupid hideout with *them* or on the porch with *them*, he's on the phone with *them*. Laughing. Howling. *Goober* this and *goober* that. One night at dinner he had a volcanic eruption. It started when his fork stopped moving and his eyes got a faraway look. Then his lips flapped and a quick snort came out.

A second later his whole face exploded. I swear, mashed potatoes shot out his nose. Mom didn't even have to tell him—he left the table and we heard him laughing in the kitchen for the next five minutes.

"What's so funny?" Dad asked me, like I must know.

I just shrugged. "Beats me."

Jake keeps saying I don't get it, and for once he's absolutely right—I don't get it. I sneaked into their famous hideout once. It's so, like, *nothing*. It's a *tree*. Sure, it's like you're under a leafy roof, but so what? What's there to *do*? All I saw were some candy wrappers and whittled sticks. It smells like hoagies.

And this goober stuff they think is so hilarious. I saw them the other day, all four of them walking down the street behind some man that seemed perfectly normal to me. Real close to him, practically clipping his heels. Then he looked back and they ran off laughing. A real riot. I had to check myself into a hospital, I was laughing so hard.

So yeah—I confess—I don't get it. But there's something he doesn't get too. He doesn't get what he's doing to me and him. To *us*. It's like he's dumping our whole past and now he's got three brothers instead of one sister. "Do *they* know how you're feeling when you're five miles away?" I say to him. "Do *they* sleepwalk to the railroad station every birthday with you? Do *they* know you're afraid of worms?" (He almost slugged me for that one.)

He just says I'm making a big deal out of nothing. He says I must be getting my hormones and they're making me goofy. He says I need a shrink.

I say I'm dumped. By my own *twin brother*.

Jake

Whatever.

So tomorrow's here and, like he said, Bump went to see if his hallucination from yesterday was real. The other three of us went straight to the hideout to wait for him first thing this morning. When he finally showed up, we were all over him.

"Didja find out, Bump?"

"Is it real, Bump?"

"What is it?"

Today Bump was back to his own cool self. He sat on the ground. He took out a piece of black licorice and started chewing. It felt funny standing over him like that, but the rest of us were too excited to sit.

"Bump—come *on*," we begged.

Bump smiled up at us. It was a face of complete satisfaction. The kind of face you get when the world lays a perfect moment on you, when everything you ever wanted in life has suddenly flopped into your lap, like I'll probably look when I get my first cell phone.

And suddenly I knew why. "Bump," I said, "you saw the best goober yet, didn't you?"

Bump looked up at me but still didn't say a word. He looked around on the ground, then held out his hand and said, "Stick."

Nacho ducked out and came back with a stick. He handed it to Bump. Bump waved us away. We stepped back. He grinned up at us and used the stick to write a word in the dirt. They were big, blocky letters like a first grader's. We're not as good as teachers at reading upside down, so we all walked around Bump and stood behind him and looked down at the word. Nobody said anything except, "Oh man," which came from Burke. We just stood there staring, as if the word was the thing itself and if we dared to breathe it might disappear.

And this was the word:

SUPERGOOBER

Lily

He says, "Twins. Twins. You're always playing the twins card. Why don't you get off it?"

I say, "It's the only card I have left. You won't even play poker with me anymore."

Jake

Supergoobers are rare. Like two-headed frogs. You're lucky if you spot one in a lifetime.

Most regular goobers have one or two funny things about them. Sometimes a goober can be sitting in class with you or walking the halls every day and you don't even know it until he goes goobery and gives himself away. This is where it's good to have somebody like Bump, who can root them out when they're not obvious. With a supergoober— you *know*. Instantly. There is nothing that is *not* funny about a supergoober.

The day you see a supergoober is a day you'll remember for the rest of your life. You'll memorize the date, like your birthday or your favorite holiday. For me July 2 will always be Supergoober Day.

His house was at the end of Meeker Street, so it had a side yard. That's where he was hammering. We sat on our bikes and watched him from across the street. (For some strange reason, until you get to know a goober, you're scared to get too close.) There was a tree. He was hammering boards under it. Even from across the street we could tell he was only hitting a nail about one out of every ten times. He didn't hammer with his arm. He hammered with his whole body, his joints flying in all different directions. Some kids, you can tell just by the way they walk or run that they're not athletes. This kid made a robot look graceful. Once he not only missed the nail—he missed the board!

Burke said, "Can't wait to see him in gym class."

Nacho said, "Who is he?"

"You mean *what* is it?" I said.

We laughed.

Nacho said, "You think his mother *made* him?"

We all knew what Nacho was talking about. The kid was wearing goggles and gloves.

"Yeah, prob'ly," said Burke. He mimicked a

mom: "You'll get flying splinters. Protect your eyes and hands."

"Okay," I said, "but any normal kid . . ."

I didn't have to finish the sentence: . . . *would take off the goggles and gloves as soon as he got out of the house.*

Then Bump said, "But . . ." He paused. We turned. He had a little grin. "Maybe his mother *didn't* make him."

Four heads turned to the kid. Burke whispered, "Holy crap."

We just stood there for a while, leaning in our bike seats, soaking in the amazement of a human being who would wear goggles and gloves. Without being told. In July.

At first we thought he was bald. Burke drifted across the street for a closer look and came back. "His hair is blond and it's cut real short." While we were thinking about that, Burke said, "That's not all."

"What?" we said.

"There's something on his shirt."

"What?"

"Mickey Mouse."

"What?"

"Mickey Mouse. He has a Mickey Mouse patch on his shirt."

We lost it. We all burst out laughing. "I didn't even think Mickey Mouse was cool when I was *three*!" Bump shouted, plenty loud enough for the kid to hear. But the kid just went on hammering. The tip of his tongue was sticking out between his lips. Supergoobers are great concentrators.

And then he did something that sent him straight to the Goober Hall of Fame. He took a handkerchief out of his back pocket, wiped his sweaty face with it, and put it back in his pocket. We had all heard of handkerchiefs. Burke said he saw one in a movie once. I remember seeing an old man in an elevator blow his nose into one a couple years ago. We just stood there gawking. You suck on a goober's amazements like you suck on candy goop from a tube. We'll never know where things might have gone from there because at that moment a side door swung open and a lady's voice called, "Ernie—lunch." And the kid—Supergoobers always listen to their mothers—dropped his hammer and ran into the house.

Lily

He's back!

Poppy!

Forever!

It started with our parents fooling us. At breakfast this morning Dad said, "We're taking you to the house." He meant the house they've been working on since spring. "We want to see if you like what we did to it."

"Okay," we said. We were impressed. They never asked our opinion before. Must mean we're practically grown-up.

So we get in the car and drive to the house and pull into the driveway. It's a little white stucco cottage with red trim and a gray roof and a porch big enough for two chairs. Jake and I are looking it over and saying stuff like, "Good work" and "Nice paint job."

Mom says, "We have one big problem. You know Dad and me. We're not musical. We don't know if we got the door chimes right. Would you mind going up and ringing the doorbell and see what you think of the sound?"

We bolted from the car, and of course I was first to the door. I pressed the button. We could hear the chimes inside. We both called back, "Sounds good."

Then the door opened.

It was Poppy! Jake and I were in a howling laughter sandwich—Poppy in front of us, parents behind. Everybody piled into the house, and pretty quick we got the story.

Poppy didn't just come for a visit last winter. He and Mom and Dad planned the whole thing. Poppy bought the old handyman special with money he'd been saving, and Mom and Dad did the work for nothing. I glared at Poppy. "You tricked us. You knew all along you were coming back." I punched him for making me cry back then, and he just laughed and swallowed Jake and me in a bear hug.

Jake

I stayed with them all morning. I stayed while we all had lunch in Poppy's new house. (We ordered pizza. There's nothing in the fridge yet.) And then I got up to leave and Lily squawked, "There he goes."

"Scrap it," I said.

"Did you see he only ate one slice of pizza? He usually eats four. He can't wait to get out of here."

I had my hand on the doorknob.

"He hates me, Poppy."

I should have left right then. I knew better. I knew she was just getting started.

The grown-ups were chuckling.

"I don't think he hates you," said Dad.

Lily plowed on. "He doesn't go riding with me anymore. We don't play cards. We don't sleep in the same room anymore. We don't do squat together."

Dad got a kick out of that one.

Lily threw her pizza down. "Yeah, laugh." She glared at them. "*You* don't know what it's like to be entangled with somebody"—boy, am I sorry Poppy ever told us we're entangled—"and then that somebody dumps you and you're left all alone with nothing to do but pick your nose." My parents' cheeks were bulging trying to hold in the laughs. Poppy looked at her like she was making sense. She jabbed a finger at me. "Look at him. He's drooling to get away. His grandfather just came here to live, and all he wants to do is go kiss Bump Stubbins. They might as well get married, since they spend all their time together. I'm surprised he still comes home to sleep."

She gave her mouth a rest for a second. Mom said, "Jake loves you, Lily."

Lily snickered. "Yeah—sure." Then as I opened the door, her question speared me: "Is that right, Jake? You love me?"

I looked at my parents, my grandfather. I pointed to my head. "She's cuckoo," I said, and went out the door.

Lily

"See?" I said. "See?"

Nobody said anything. They just stared at me.
Mom and Dad actually had little grins, which
made no sense. Me? I was feeling great. Why not? I
was *right*! For two seconds. Then I started bawling.

Jake

Meeker Street. They were at the curb, same as yesterday.

"Where were you?" said Bump. "We went to your house and knocked."

"At my grandpa's," I said. "He just came to live here." I looked across the street. "Where is he?"

"In for lunch," said Burke.

"So what's happening?"

"Same old," said Bump. "He's hammering away. Still don't know we're here." He shook his head. "Unbefreakinglievable."

"In his own little world," said Nacho.

"That's how they are," said Bump.

It's true: goobers live in their own little world. Planet Goober. They don't seem to notice anything else. If the whole rest of the world is wearing black shoes and they're the only one on the planet wearing yellow shoes, they won't even notice. Or care.

And that leads to another thing about goobers, probably the mainest thing of all: *goobers don't know they're goobers*. They just skip happily along through life thinking they're perfectly normal.

Just then Soop—that's what we call him now—came back outside and for the first time in two days looked across the street and noticed us. He had a glass of something in his hand. He called, "Hi, guys!" He held up the glass. "Want some lemonade?"

Our knees buckled. Burke let out one quick snort bomb, but the rest of us did a pretty good job of swallowing the laughs. For a good reason. When a goober says something totally hilarious, you naturally want to bust out laughing. But if you're smart, you make sure to hold it in and keep paying attention, because while you're busy laughing you might miss the next gem that comes along.

And here's another rule: act like they're normal. If you don't, if you explode a volcano of laugh lava like you feel like doing, you might spook them. You might cause them to see themselves the way you do. The last thing you want is for a goober to all of a sudden look in the mirror one day and say, *Well whaddaya know—I'm a goober!* Of course, that's probably not going to happen. But still, you don't want to take chances. Supergoobers are too rare. You don't want to risk losing them. So you keep your face straight and act normal. Even though the kid just called across the street to perfect strangers, "Hi, guys! Want some lemonade?" *And* was wearing an orange hat. *Orange.*

Yeah, it takes a *lot* of discipline.

So Nacho answered, "Hi, Soop!" I cringed but the kid didn't even notice the "Soop."

And Bump said, "No thanks. We're just sitting here watching. Whatcha makin'?"

The kid beamed. "A clubhouse." He took a swig of his lemonade. He beamed again. "Hey, guys— want to be in the club?"

Bump rolled across the street. The rest of us followed but hung back. Let the master work it.

"What club?" said Bump.

"My club," said the kid.

"What's it called?" said Bump.

"I don't know yet," said the kid. "Maybe you guys can help me pick a name."

"Who's in the club now?" said Bump.

The kid threw out his arms. "Me!" He stuck out his hand. "I forgot to introduce myself. I'm Ernest. But you can call me Ernie."

They shook. "You can call me Bump." He pointed to each of us. "And you can call him Burke. And that there is Nacho. And that's Jake."

Of course Ernie couldn't let it go at that. He had to shake hands with each of us and say, "Nice to meet you."

"So Ernie," Bump went on, "if we joined up, then there would be five of us. From what I can see, Ernie"—he pretended to study the woody mess—"it doesn't look like it would be big enough."

"No problemo," said Ernie. Again the arms flew out. "I'll make it bigger!"

"Wow," said Bump, acting impressed. "Really?"

"Sure. I can make it as big as I want. My dad will get me more wood. Look"—he held up a yellow plastic bucket, like a little kid would take to the beach—"I have enough nails to make a skyscraper!" He laughed.

"Wow, Ernie," said Bump. "You're really some-thin'." Bump turned to us. "What do you think, fellas? Do you think we oughta join Ernie's club?"

You had to see Bump's face. It was as serious as if he was answering a question in English class—which only made the whole thing funnier. It was too much for Nacho. He pedaled off up the street, gagging on his own laughs.

As for me, I understood exactly what was going on. It's one thing to observe a goober, it's totally something else to interact with one. The key is to interact with the goober so he doesn't suspect anything fishy is going on. Which, with goobers, is easy, because they're so gullible and agreeable. So you act all serious and string them along. You don't just nod and say "Yep" and "That's nice." You give them a nudge. You steer them in a direc-tion that will bring out their gooberness in all its glory. I knew that's what Bump was doing.

So I spoke up. "Sure, Bump. Sounds like a good idea." I rolled my bike alongside his. "Let's join up."

"Yeah," said Burke, coasting over. "Let's do it."

Soop let out a little yelp-cheer. "Yes!" He did

something that he probably thought was a happy dance but actually looked like somebody fighting off a swarm of bees. When he finally calmed down, he said, "So guys, care to help? We could consolidate our efforts. I can find some more hammers."

Care to help . . . consolidate our efforts. This guy was getting better by the minute. "Nah, sorry, Ernie," said Bump, and he really sounded sorry. "We'd consolidate if we could, but we all have blisters on our hands and our doctor told us no hammering for a month."

Burke started choke-laughing. He headed off to join Nacho.

"Oh—okay," said the kid. "No problemo, señors."

Goobers believe everything you tell them.

"So you go ahead and hammer away," said Bump. "We'll just hang here and watch you for a while. If you don't mind."

"Heck no, I don't mind," the kid chirped, and dived right back into Planet Goober. He put on his goggles, put on his gloves, and started pounding away.

Lily

Don't worry, he loves you, they said.

He had an audience, they said. He was uncomfortable.

He's being a boy, they said.

Okay, I figured, with the audience he wasn't himself. Give him a second chance. Maybe a boy isn't so much a boy when you catch him in his room.

I waited till after dark. He was on his back on his bed, reading an X-Men comic. I had hardly stepped into the room when he said, "What?" Actually he didn't *say* it. He *snarled* it. Practically spit it. *What's the use*, I figured. I went back to my room.

I stood before the poster on my wall. It shows

a California Zephyr from the 1950s, way before we were born. Two engines pulling, silver with red faces and red stripes down the sides. Sleepers. Coaches. Dining car. Sightseeing dome car. I counted thirteen cars in all. Crossing the empty, endless Great Salt Flats somewhere in Utah. We were there, Jake and me, right *there*, crossing the flats just like the passengers behind the black windows in the poster. The sway of the train. The click of the wheels. I got a chill.

Jake

Supergoobers are like hot peppers. Or staring at the sun. You can't take too much at once.

So we busted back to the hideout and spent the rest of the day hooting and replaying every moment. We were sitting in a circle.

"Care to help!"

"Consolidate our efforts!"

"Hi, guys!"

"Want some lemonade!"

"Hi, Soop! I can't believe you said that."

"He never noticed."

"Wow, Ernie—you're really somethin'. That was awesome, Bump. How'd you keep a straight face?"

"We can't help—we got blisters!"

We laughed so hard our stomachs hurt.

Then questions came.

"How did he get that way?"

"He was born that way."

"Don't parents have something to do with it?"

"Every goober I knew, their parents were perfectly normal."

"What if a supergoober has a brother or sister? Would they be supergoobers too?"

"I got a cousin who's a goober. Some days he's even a supergoober." This was Bump talking. We were all ears. "He has two sisters, my girl cousins. And they're normal. I mean, for girls."

"So," said Nacho, "there's five people in the family and only one is a goober?"

"Right," said Bump.

"So," said Burke, giving Bump the sly eye, "there's a goober in your family."

Bump stared at Burke. "Yeah. You got a problem?"

"Me?" said Burke. "*I* ain't got no problem."

"So *I* do?" said Bump.

"Hey—you said it, not me. There's a goober in your family."

Nacho poked Burke. "So what're you saying?"

Burke shrugged. "I'm saying, ever hear of genes?"

Nacho's brain couldn't take it. "Huh?"

Personally, I was getting a kick out of all this. I spoke up. "Burke says maybe gooberism runs in a family. Even though Bump isn't a goober, maybe he's got a little bit of goober blood in him."

Suddenly I was in the dirt. Bump had stuck his foot in my back and pushed me over. I got up laughing, but I was the only one. Bump looked like he wanted to jab a stick down my throat. "It don't run in the family," he said.

"Cool," I said, sitting back up. "Tell Burke. He's the one who said genes. Look at him." I pointed. "Look at his face. He can't stop grinning. He's jukin' you, man. Chill out." I poked Bump. "Take a joke, dude."

Nacho got us back on track. He made goggle circles over his eyes with his fingers and chirped, "No problemo, señors."

We picked up our laughing where we left off.

Lily

"Why?"

I must have said that word a thousand times this week. And I'm still waiting for an answer from Poppy.

Oh, he's given me answers to a lot of little whys.

Like "Why does Jake need his own room?"

"Because your parents said so."

"Why?"

"Because you're getting older."

"What's that have to do with it?"

"Maybe Jake shouldn't be getting undressed in front of you."

"I won't look."

"He's a boy and you're a girl."

"No we're not."

"Oops, my mistake."

It was the day after Jake walked out. We were sitting on Poppy's living room floor. There was no furniture yet. We were playing poker. Our money was the dried beetles Poppy collected from around the world. It's the only thing he has a lot of.

"Poppy," I said, "you *know* what I mean. You're missing the point. We're not a *regular* boy and girl. We're brother and sister. And we're not regular brother and sister. We're twins. And we're not even regular twins. We're *special*." I squeezed his finger. "You know what I mean, Poppy. You're the only other person who totally *knows*."

He smiled, nodded, patted my hand. "I know. Raise you one beetle."

"You know about the snow fort and the bruises. You know about the day at the beach. You know about our birthday and the train station. You know about goombla."

He patted. "I know . . . I know. . . ."

"So?" I said.

"So what?"

"So why?"

"Why what?"

"Why everything? Why won't Jake ride and play with me anymore or even hardly talk to me? Why did he change? Why is he so different now? Where did our goombla go? Raise you two beetles and call you."

"That's a lot of whys—and one where."

"So give me a lot of answers."

"How about if I give you one? One answer fits all."

"Give it."

"He's a boy. Three jacks."

"Bull," I said. "Four queens." I took the pot.

He shrugged. He got up. "Let's go shopping. I need furniture."

"Poppy, you *have* to have an answer. You're old. Old people have the answers."

"Ask me tomorrow," he said. "Maybe I'll have a better answer then."

So we went to Goodwill and got him some furniture. And he got a secondhand bike till he can afford his own car. And he looked for a job. I went with him the next day and the next. And every day, as soon as he opened the front door, I said, "Why?" And every day he said, "He's a boy."

Until today, when he said, "Maybe you're asking the wrong question."

I got excited. "What's the right question?"

"I don't know," he said.

I pounded his chest and buried my face in his shirt and pretended I was bawling, but part of me wasn't pretending.

Jake

As I said before, it's not enough to just observe a goober. You have to mess with him. You *have* to.

So day after day we pulled up to the curb at Soop's house and we watched him hammer and saw away in his orange hat. He asked how our blisters were coming along, and we told him they were still pretty bad and we acted all sad because we couldn't help him build the clubhouse.

We asked him tons of questions, just to keep him talking. He was our daily entertainment. Better than the movies. For instance, when we asked him what his favorite subject was, he said, "Oh, I would say mathematics." Not just *Math*. But *Oh, I would say mathematics*. Classic goober answer.

If we didn't get a good goober answer right away, we kept digging.

"Do you have a girlfriend?"

"No."

"Why not?"

"I'm still a little young for that."

"You like girls, don't you?"

"Sure."

"Why?"

"They're people. I like all people."

"Do you think girls are as good as boys?"

"Absolutely. I believe in gender equality."

Bingo! *I believe in gender equality.* It's like digging for night crawlers. If you keep at it, sooner or later you'll come to a beaut.

Our questions got sillier and sillier.

"How many bites does it take you to finish a hamburger?"

"Where would you wipe your nose if you forgot your handkerchief?"

"Did you ever pee while standing on your head?"

By now we didn't even try to hide it. We were hooting and howling at the stuff he said, and he was laughing right along. Goobers don't know when they're being laughed at. They just think they're funny.

I've been thinking about it, and here's the thing. A true goober—you can't insult him. You can't hurt him. Physically, sure. But that's all. So go ahead, mess with him. Insult him. Mock him. Embarrass him. Boo him. Everything rolls off the inhabitants of Planet Goober. They're invincible.

Anyway, that's how it went—until today. Somewhere along the line Bump asked him where he moved here from and he said, "Gary, Indiana," and Bump said, "Did you like it there?" and he said, "Yes," and Bump said, "So why did you leave?" and there was no answer.

We were all so shocked, it took a minute to reach our brains: *He didn't answer.* It's totally ungoober-like to not answer a question. He just went on hammering. "Must not've heard," Bump whispered. So Bump said, "Ernie?"

The hammer stopped. Ernie cocked his head. That's another thing he does—he cocks his head when you say his name or ask a question, like he's moving his ear to scoop up every last sound wave from your voice. So he cocks his head and says, "Hello?"

And Bump says, "I guess you didn't hear me. I asked you why you moved away from Gary, Indiana."

And Soop just stares at Bump. Stares and blinks, stares and blinks. Then he suddenly jumps up and says, "Oops, I just remembered, guys. I have to go in and do something for my mother." He runs for the door. "Seeya later!"

We all looked at each other, like, *Huh?* We hung around for a couple minutes to make sure he wasn't coming back out. As we coasted up the street we started talking.

"He's lying," said Bump.

We all agreed.

"Unbelievable," said Nacho. Because goobers don't lie.

"And he acted like he didn't hear you the first time," said Burke, "but he did. So that's like a lie too."

We pedaled for a while, trying to make sense of it. I figured I might as well ask the obvious question. "So why's he lying?"

We came up with lots of theories:

His father is in the mob and they're in witness protection.

His mother is a shoplifter and they were kicked out of Indiana.

His parents lost their jobs and had to move.

Soop has allergies (most goobers have allergies) and Indiana was bad for his health.

Soop is a firebug and they had to get out before he was caught.

They lost their house in a flood.

Or an earthquake.

Or termites.

Soop is a shoplifter.

We stopped to pick up hoagies and went to the hideout and kept making theories. Most of them were just silly and we didn't believe them ourselves. We were mostly just laughing and scratching our heads over the whole thing, but then I started to notice something. The longer the list of theories got, the more it bothered us that we didn't know the real answer. Then Burke said something. It seems pretty innocent, even now when I think of it and write it down. He said, "It was just a simple question." That's all. "It was just a simple question." But now that I look back on it, and I remember his face as he said it and the sharp edge in his voice, I think maybe that was the moment things turned in a different direction. Because then the guys started saying stuff like:

"Yeah, a simple question. 'Why did you move here?'"

"So why can't he answer? Don't we deserve an answer?"

"He didn't have to go in and do something for his mother. He made that up."

"He lied."

"We come over every day. We keep him company. Look what he does."

"He lies to us."

By the time we were done saying all this, something had changed. Soop was still funny, but funny wasn't the *only* thing he was. Something else was in there too, I wasn't sure what. Then Bump said, "He didn't just lie. He lied to the Death Rays."

There it was. It was like the last skinny sunbeam went behind a cloud and the sky was dark and getting darker and you knew you better pedal for home before you got wet.

And then Bump rolled his hoagie paper into a ball and threw it across the hideout and said, "He's gonna pay."

Lily

"I'm getting scared," I told Poppy.

We were in his kitchen. He was making me a PB&J sandwich. Without the J. He forgot to get jelly. There are lots of things his house doesn't have yet.

So he said, "This about your brother by any chance?"

I told him it was.

He handed me the sandwich. "Milk?"

"Yes, please," I said. "Do you have chocolate syrup by any chance?"

"Sorry," he said. "So—it seems like you were mad at first. Then sad." He gave me a glass of milk. "Now you're scared?"

I stared at my lunch. "Yeah."

"How so?"

"We're writing our journals, you know? Like you said?"

"Right. Good."

"Well, we always kind of knew what the other one was writing. But now I don't know. I, like, try to tune in to him. But I can't."

"Eat your sandwich."

"I'm not hungry."

"I'm not going to talk to you unless you eat."

I took a bite. "Talk."

"So why does that scare you?"

"Because it means I'm losing him."

He chuckled. "You're not losing him."

"I'm glad *you* think it's funny."

He came over to my chair, lifted me off, sat down, and plunked me onto his lap. "I don't think it's funny. I just think you're wrong, that's all. You're never going to lose him. He'll always be your brother. This is just a phase."

I pounded the table. "Phase, my hiney. It's bad enough he doesn't want to be around me anymore. But now our goombla is starting to go away." I quick turned to look into his face. Our noses bumped. "Poppy . . ." In his eyes I found all the love there was, and still it wasn't enough. "Poppy, we're becoming untangled!" I was crying again.

He hugged me and rocked me for a while. He put the sandwich in front of my face. Finally I took another bite.

"I'd wipe your tears with a napkin," he said, "except I don't have napkins."

"You don't have anything," I sniveled. "Who ever heard of a house without jelly?"

"Let me know when you're finished feeling sorry for yourself," he said. "I have something to say."

I wanted to grump for a year, but I only lasted a minute. "Okay," I said finally, "what do you have to say?"

He tapped the table twice with his fingernail. "I think I know your problem."

"Big deal," I said. "I know it too. It's *him*."

"I don't think so," he said. "I think"—he pointed—"it's you."

I sneered. "Right, Poppy. I'm being dumped by my own brother and it's my fault."

He stared at me for a long time, squinting, then

he said, "You know what you need?"

"I can't wait," I said. "What?"

"A life."

"Huh?"

"You need a life."

I looked around. I couldn't find a mirror. I pulled at my shirt. I poked my stomach. "Isn't this me? Aren't I real? Alive? What am I—a ghost?"

"You're too wrapped up in your brother. You need a life of your own. Not a Lily-and-Jake life. A Lily life."

"But you're the one who said we're entangled. Now you're telling me I'm too wrapped up in him? Did you lie to us before?"

"No, I didn't lie." He got up. He sat on the edge of the table. "It's true, there is something very special between you and Jake. And it will always be there. But you can't allow it to stop you from becoming your own person. There's a life waiting for you away from Jake. You need to find it."

I turned away. I looked out the window. I saw backyards and fences and houses and sky. I remembered the day at the beach: Jake and me secretly grinning under our parents' scolding, knowing we weren't really lost, knowing—even if we were at opposite ends of the universe—we could never be lost. I tried to imagine life away from Jake. I couldn't.

I turned to Poppy. He was getting blurry. I felt my lip quiver. I croaked, "I don't have a life!"

Jake

All of a sudden some of that funny stuff about Soop doesn't seem so funny anymore. It's like we see him with different eyes now. Yesterday he made us laugh. Today he makes us mad.

But I don't think it's happening just because Soop didn't answer a question. Let's face it, he didn't really lie to us. Okay, maybe, technically, it was a lie about having to go see his mother, but that's a pretty harmless lie. And knowing how honest most goobers are, I wouldn't be surprised if it was true.

No, the fact is, whether he did or didn't answer some question, sooner or later this was going to happen. It happens with all of them. I can't explain it. For once, don't blame the goober. The goober never changes. He still says *ahnt* instead of *aunt*. Or he still wears a beaded belt with reindeer on it. Or he still can't bounce a basketball twice in a row. No, it's not the goober. The goober is forever. It's you. It's you who changes. Something inside you that used to tickle—now it feels like a pinch. You're done laughing. You just want to smack him.

So today it was different as we parked at Soop's house. For one thing, we were now off the street and on the sidewalk. And we were calling him Soop right to his face. Of course, goobers being goobers, he probably didn't even notice.

We got an early taste of the new deal when Soop looked up from his work, which today was digging holes. He said, "So guys, how are those blisters coming along? Ready to jump in yet?"

And Bump said, "Nah. We ain't jumpin' in."

Soop looked surprised—"Oh"—and then sympathetic. "Boy, you guys must have yourselves some awful blisters. Do they really hurt bad?"

"Nah," said Bump. "They don't hurt at all. In fact, we don't even have blisters."

I could see Soop getting a little confused. "Oh . . . well . . . that's good."

"Yeah, that's good," said Bump. "In fact we never did have blisters. We just told you that. We lied."

Now Soop was standing there blinking at us—goobers blink a lot—the spade hanging in his hand. All he could say was, "Oh."

"Yeah, we didn't want to help, so we made up that lie about the blisters. We'd rather just sit here and watch you do all the work."

Burke picked it up. "Yeah, Soop, and then when you're done making the clubhouse, we'll all move in with ya."

At that point a normal person would have sneered and said, "Yeah, right," and thrown the hammer at us, not to mention a mouthful of choice words. But goobers. . . goobers are like sponges. They take all the crap you throw at them and just soak it up and nothing comes back. So Soop just breaks out this massive grin and pumps his fist and says, "Yes!" As if the only thing he heard was *we'll all move in with ya*.

Nacho jumped in. "Hey, Soop, how come you wear goggles and gloves?"

Soop jammed the spade into the ground. "To

protect my hands and eyes," he said.

"Did your mommy make you wear them?"

"I wouldn't say she *made* me," he said. "She suggested it. And I thought it was a good idea, so"—he held up his gloved hands so all the world could see—"I did it!"

I had been holding back, but now the words just came blurting out: "You da man, Soop!" And he gave a fist pump and another "Yes!" And I'm thinking, *Hey, yeah, I can do this.*

"But Soop," said Burke, "nobody else would be caught dead wearing gloves and goggles. Don't you feel like a dork?"

And Soop actually leaned on the spade for a second and frowned like he was seriously thinking over the question. Then he gave a quick snap of his head and said, "Nope," and went back to digging.

That's how it went, us asking dumb question after dumb question. If you could compare it to a boxing match, we were jabbing him in the nose—*bam bam bam bam*—round after round.

"Hey, Soop—you look bald. Why don't you let your hair grow a little?"

"Hey, Soop—where's your Mickey Mouse shirt?"

"Hey, Soop—is everybody as cool as you where you came from?"

"Hey, Soop—where did you get that hankie from? Your grandpa? Is it fulla boogers?"

And Soop—bless his little goober heart—he answered every question all serious like it was on a test.

Lily

Poppy says there's two of me. There's the Jake-and-Lily me. And there's the Just Lily me. It's the Just Lily me who needs a life. Because right now she's nobody.

"So how does Just Lily get a life?" I asked him. I was combing Poppy's long white hair. I had pulled the rubber band off the ponytail.

Poppy thought about it. "Attitude," he said. "I think it starts with that. Attitude."

"Don't I already have attitude?" I said.

"The Jake-and-Lily you does," he said. "But Just Lily? She's"—his hands went thumbs-down—"*fssst*."

"What's *fssst*?" I said.

"Blah. Empty. Zip. Zero. Nada."

"There's a lot of ways to say nothing," I said.

He nodded. "I should know. I was nothing for a long time."

The comb went through his hair a lot easier than it goes through mine—when I comb it once a month. "Was that after Grandma died?" I said.

"It was," he said. "Bad time for your Poppy."

"So how did you get out of it? Did you get attitude?"

He thought. He nodded. "Yeah, I guess I did, come to think of it."

"Do you have another rubber band?" I said. "So what attitude did you get?"

He found me another rubber band. "Well, I guess it started with getting mad. I got mad."

"Mad? What at?"

"Me. Myself."

"Why?"

He thought some more. I felt like my combing was helping him think. "I'm remembering a day in Cape Town. That's South Africa. I had a day off but I hadn't even left the boat. I was standing at the rail, looking over the harbor. Lots of little sailboats, like white butterflies. Then comes this speedboat.

Zoom! Right through all the butterflies. I watched it till it went out of sight. It never turned. Never slowed down. Making a beeline to somewhere. And, I don't know, something just clicked inside me. Like, *Hey pal, he's going somewhere.* Somewhere. *He's* alive." Poppy shrugged. "Next thing I knew, I was mad at myself. Not sure why. Because I was a butterfly and not a speedboat, I guess. I went down to the docks and walked into the city. Ate me some wild oysters. Really just . . . walked. Walked. Watched. Listened. Smelled. Came alive. I worked my way straight back to California and called your mom and dad and told them I was coming here to live. All because I saw a speedboat. What are you doing up there?"

I looked down. I started laughing. I guess I was listening so hard to Poppy I didn't notice what I was doing to his hair. It was now in twin pop-up pigtails. Without a mirror, all he could do was feel around up there. "How's it look?" he said.

"Fabulous," I told him. "So Poppy, what are you saying? If I want a life of my own, I need to go to South Africa?"

He shook his head, which shook his pop-up

pigtails. "You need to get mad. Start with that. Yesterday you said you were scared. Mad is better than scared."

"What do I get mad at?"

He pulled me around in front of him. He pointed between my eyes.

"Me?" I said.

"Who else? It worked for me."

"How do I do it?"

"That's where attitude comes in," he said. "You gotta say to yourself, 'Hey, girl, wise up. Look at your brother. He's off having a great ol' time with his pals. He doesn't need you. And look at you. All you're doing is crying because your big bad brother won't play with you. Boohoo. Where's your self-respect? Toughen up, girl.'" He gave me a little arm punch. I punched him back. He grinned. "Now you're talkin'."

So off we went to do some shopping at the strip of stores three blocks away. Since we were walking we could only buy as much as we could carry. We got blackberry jelly, chocolate syrup, a used egg-shaped mirror, duct tape, flashlight, batteries, and some other stuff. I kept saying to myself *Wise up, girl . . . wise up . . . ya big baby. . . .*

As we were unloading the bags back at the house, I said, "It's not working."

"What's not?" he said.

"Getting mad at myself. I've been trying for a couple hours now. I can't seem to get the hang of it."

He wagged the chocolate syrup. "Want some?"

"Yes," I said.

"Maybe I was wrong. Maybe you're aiming at the wrong target."

"What's the right target?"

He grinned. "Guess."

"Jake?"

"The one and only."

He made my chocolate milk and set it on the table. "But I'm already mad at him," I said.

"I'll bet you could get madder."

I took a sip. "You think so?"

"Sure. You might only be using twenty percent of your mad capacity. I'll bet you have a lot left in you."

I drank. I thought about it. "But Poppy, wouldn't that be dangerous? If I used up all my mad on him, I could blow up what's left of our goombla."

He chuckled and shook his head. "No way. You still love him, don't you—even though you're mad at him?"

"Yes."

"Exactly. And the more you love someone, the safer it is to be mad at them. Love can handle mad, no problem."

"Cool," I said. And I thought, *Get ready, Jake. You got an avalanche of mad coming your way.*

I was starting to feel a little flicker of a life already.

Jake

I guess every once in a while you have a day you just want to toss in the trash can. This was one.

As my parents were getting up from the breakfast table this morning, my mother looked at me and said, "I'd like you to go riding with your sister today."

I was just chomping into an apple strudel Pop-Tart. I looked up in midchomp. "Huh?"

"Go riding with your sister today."

I stared at her.

"I'm waiting for you to nod your head," she said. "That'll mean you heard me."

"Why?" I said.

She hitched on her tool belt. "I just think it would be nice. Won't kill you."

"But *why*?" I think I screeched.

She put her hands on the back of Lily's chair. Lily looked as stunned as I did.

"Because I think you're going a little overboard with these new friends of yours. Morning, noon, and night. I can't remember the last time I saw you two together. I miss it. Do it for me. That enough reasons?"

I shrugged. "Fine. I'll go riding with her."

She stared at me. She gave a chuckle. She tweaked my nose. "Jakey, Jakey. You almost got me."

"What?" I said.

"You're going to listen to me, aren't you? You're going to ride with her to the end of the block and back. One minute of your time, right?"

"I'm not a babysitter," I said.

"No," she said, "you're a brother. And you're starting to make me mad because you think it will kill you to spend a little time with your sister." She was glaring at me now. "So here's what you're gonna do. I'm not asking you now. I'm telling you. You're gonna spend the whole day with her."

My sister and I both shrieked. *"What?"*

Her pointing finger was aimed between my

eyes. "The. Whole. Day. Do not let her out of your sight."

Was this really happening? "Mom, you're taking her side. You're believing all this crap she's saying."

Lily whined, "Mom, I don't even *want* to."

Mom swung to her. "Don't *you* start." She took a final swig of orange juice. "You have your orders."

She went out the door. And came back. Stuck her head in the kitchen. "Be very, very careful." She kind of sang it with a smile and was gone. That's when I knew there was no way out. You don't mess with that smile and voice. I never finished my Pop-Tart.

So started the longest day of my life.

We cleaned up the kitchen after we ate. When our mother says, "Be very, very careful," we're never sure exactly what she's referring to. So to be on the safe side, we just make sure we're perfect for that day. Meaning we do all our jobs: clean up the kitchen after meals, make our beds, pick up our rooms, brush our teeth, put the toothpaste caps back on, check the porch for UPS deliveries.

Then we headed off on our bikes. At the end of the block I turned right, she turned left. In the first instant I thought, *Great! I'm rid of her!* In the second instant I remembered: *Do not let her out of your sight.* I U-turned and went after her.

And that's pretty much how it went. She led me all over town, like I was her puppy or slave or something. I prayed she wouldn't go past Ernie the goober's house. I didn't want the guys to see what had happened to me. My prayers were answered.

Around noon she headed for Bert's Deli. She got a cheese hoagie with hot peppers and an orange Crush. I got nothing. Because, stupid idiot that I am, I didn't bring any money with me. We sat at one of the little round tables in front of Bert's. She unwrapped the hoagie real slow. She looked at it. Smelled it. A drop of olive oil glistened in the sun. She licked it away. The hoagie was cut in half. She took about ten minutes to decide which half she would eat first. By now the hoagie smell was seeping into my bones. My elbows were smelling it. I would have paid two months' allowance for a cheese hoagie with hot peppers. She took the first bite. She chewed and chewed and chewed. I died. About twenty people went in and out of Bert's before she even got to the second half. When she finally finished, she licked the paper, wrapped it into a ball, and finished off her orange Crush. Then, like suddenly she changed from a snail to a squirrel, she shot out of her seat, tossed away the can and paper, and jumped onto her bike.

She headed for home. She turned on the downstairs TV. She put on one of her DVDs of *The Gray Shadow*. It's a stupid cops-and-robbers show for kids. She thinks she's going to be a detective. After five minutes I couldn't take any more. I was on my way out when I heard her say Mom's words from the morning: "Don't let her out of your sight." I came back. She has ten *Gray Shadow* episodes. I had to watch every one of them. When I heard Mom and Dad coming in the kitchen door, I went upstairs and slammed my door.

Lily

I went to Poppy's for breakfast. We sat at the kitchen table. I would have had toast and blackberry jelly except there was no toaster. So it was jelly on bread. I would have had hot chocolate except there was no microwave. So it was cold chocolate milk. Poppy was sipping coffee.

"It's not working," I told him.

"I think I heard this before," he said.

"I tried," I said. "All day yesterday. Mom made us stay together. I was mad at him all day. I ate my lunch in front of him and didn't share a bite while he was starving. I made him watch my *Gray Shadow* DVDs. I didn't speak to him all day."

"Not a word?"

"Not a word. And I thought it was working.

And then I got up this morning and—*fssst*. Zippo. No mad. It was gone."

Poppy sighed. "I guess you just don't have what it takes."

I sighed. "Guess not." I finished my bread in silence. "What's wrong with me, Poppy?"

He squeezed my hand. "Not a thing. You're just too nice, that's all."

"So what now?"

"Well," he said, "at least we learned something. We know mad doesn't work for you. So we need to find another way to get you a life." He sipped and stared at me, as if there was an answer somewhere on my face. "How about"—he stared some more—"a friend."

"I have friends," I told him.

"I mean a best friend. Like girls always seem to have in books and movies. Somebody you're on the phone with as soon as you wake up. Always sleeping over at each other's house. Shopping the malls together. Somebody you just can't live without."

I said, "Does the name *Jake* ring a bell?"

"This isn't about Jake. It's about Just Lily."

"Sorry."

I told him I have friends in school and in the neighborhood. I talk to them and we do stuff and we have fun and I like them. But I never slept over. And I *can* live without them.

"Pick one out," he said. "The one you like best."

I thought about it. "Well, Anna Matuzak, I guess. She lives a block away. She's in my grade. We both like Reese's Pieces. And purple."

He slapped the table. "Sounds like a match. Call her up. Invite her for a sleepover."

I wish Poppy would take things a little slower. I'm getting woozy. But I did what he said. I didn't just call Anna Matuzak. I rode to her house. Her mother came to the door. She said Anna was out swimming somewhere. I asked if Anna could come for a sleepover. Her mother looked surprised. She said my invitation was "very nice" and she would ask Anna as soon as she got home. As I was walking away she said, "Oh, and honey, I'm sorry but I have to ask—what's your name?"

"Lily Wambold," I said.

Anna called after dinner. She sounded surprised too, but she said, "Sure, I'll come."

So it's set. Tomorrow night a friend is coming

to sleep over. Mom and Dad said no problem. They said we can order pizza. We can watch DVDs. We can stay up as late as we want—"as long as you're not going wild," said Dad.

I'm planning the whole night. I feel myself getting excited. All of a sudden Anna Matuzak is the biggest thing in my life.

Jake

What happened yesterday?

I felt like I missed the first half of a great movie. I tore my Pop-Tart out of the toaster and ate it on my bike. We always meet at the hideout first thing in the morning, but no one was there yet. I waited as long as I could—about thirty seconds—and pedaled for Meeker Street.

I could see the word from a block away, but even when I pulled up close I couldn't believe it. It was painted across the wall of the clubhouse in thick yellow letters:

SOOP

Soop must have put the roof on yesterday,

because the clubhouse looked finished—if *finished* is the word. The ends of the wallboards were sticking out past the corners and were diving this way and that. The whole thing was slanted to the right as if it was falling into a sinkhole. If my parents saw it, they'd either croak or laugh for a week. It looked like it belonged in a cartoon. And that's not even counting the giant yellow word.

I felt a little uncomfortable, being the only one on the scene so early in the morning. So I did a loop around town. When I came back the kid was outside, staring at the word. I didn't want to deal with this, but the kid saw me U-turning and called, "Hey, Jake!"

Drat, I thought. I don't know why I didn't just keep going. You never ever let a goober call the shots. I guess it was hearing my name.

"Hey," I said. I pulled to the curb. "What's up?" I felt funny talking to him without the guys around. I missed Bump leading the way.

He pointed. "Look what somebody did, Jake."

I pretended like I hadn't noticed before. "Wow," I said.

He walked over to me. I was really uncomfortable now. He had never been so close. He leaned on my handlebars. "That's me. Soop. The nickname you guys call me."

He knows! I thought.

"Think so?" I said.

He nodded. "Yeah. I think so. But"—he zeroed in on me—"the big question is, who did it? And why?"

He didn't seem mad or upset. Just curious.

"Beats me," I said, looking around—where were the guys? "Maybe just some kids goofing off. Summer vacation, y'know?"

"Nothing better to do," he said.

"Yeah."

"A prank."

"Yeah."

And then I heard Nacho's war cry, "Death Rays forever!" and the guys were busting down the street. They pulled up at the curb and they all did just like me—they pretended nothing was wrong. I'm sure they rehearsed it.

"Hey, Erno—nice clubhouse."

"Way to go, dude!"

"You da hammer!"

You could see the compliments sinking into him. "Thanks, guys. It was my first construction venture, so I guess it's okay. But"—he pointed— "what do you think of that word?"

"Looks great to me, Erno," said Bump. "Nice paint job."

"I like the yellow," said Burke.

"But I didn't do it," said Soop.

"You *didn't*?" said Bump, and I knew from the fake shock on his face that he was the one. "So who did it?"

Soop snapped his fingers. "Bump, *that's* the question." Still not mad, just curious. "I mean, you're the only guys who call me Soop. I wonder who else knows my nickname is Soop."

Bump pretended to study the clubhouse in a new light. "Golly gee, Erno. Beats me."

Soop gave me a shoulder pat. "Jake thinks it was just kids playing a prank."

"Hoodlum kids," sneered Burke.

"Nothin' better to do," sneered Nacho.

Soop snapped his fingers. "That's *exactly* what Jake said." It was almost like he was starting to enjoy being vandalized. But that's typical of goobers too. You dump crap on them and they think it's roses. "Or maybe"—he laughed—"they were trying to write the S-O-U-P soup and they can't even spell it right!"

Five kids howling with laughter, only four at the same thing.

Then Bump was wagging his head. "I don't know . . . I don't know. . . ."

"What, Bump?" goes Soop.

"I got another theory," said Bump.

"What's that?" Soop was all ears. Fascinated.

"I think it's just somebody telling you how beautiful your clubhouse is and they think it would be even better if you painted it yellow."

Soop's eyes widened. He gave the shack a long look. "You think so?"

Bump nodded. "Yep. I think so."

Soop seemed to study Bump for a minute. Then he looked at the rest of us. "Can I ask you guys a question?" he said.

"Ask away," I heard myself say.

"How come you guys call me Soop? It's the first time I ever had a nickname, but I don't know where it comes from."

The four of us looked at each other, like we were flipping a ball back and forth. The silence was making me nervous. "No big deal," I told him. "It just means 'cool' around here."

Nacho picked it up. "Yeah. I guess you didn't have that word in Gary, Indiana."

"It's short," said Bump, "for 'super kid.'"

Soop beamed. "Neato!"

Lily

The sleepover stunk.

Anna Matuzak—what a bimbo. All night she complained that the pizza didn't have extra cheese. "I *always* get extra cheese . . . I *always* get extra cheese." She said it a thousand times. But that didn't stop her from eating six of the eight slices.

When she wasn't complaining and eating, she was looking at herself in my mirror. She brought a purple suitcase with her, and inside that suitcase was *another* purple (she calls it "lavender") suitcase. A little square *purple* one. It was full of cosmetics. She shoved my stuff aside and laid it all out. Suddenly my room was a beauty salon. Or, in her case, ugly salon. She crapped up everything above her neck except her ears. When I clamped her eyelash curler onto the end of my nose, she screamed and took it to the bathroom and scrubbed it. When she finished with her face she painted her fingernails. "It's Lovely Lavender," she snooted, holding the bottle out to me like I was supposed to kiss it. Then she did her toenails. She was a vision in Poopy Purple. She said I should use a toothpick to get the dirt out from under my nails.

Just to pry her away from my mirror, I took her down to the basement to my train place. It's just a bookcase, for now. Someday I'm going to make a whole display on a Ping-Pong table. I showed her my yellow-and-red caboose with the off-duty engineer waving out the window. I showed her my Pennsylvania Railroad Vista Dome car. I showed her my Southern Crescent Pullman Palace sleeper. I showed her my B&O hopper complete with tiny coal pieces from a chunk I smashed on the sidewalk with a hammer. When I told her she could touch the coal, she made a face and said, "No way!" and raced back upstairs to the mirror.

"Wanna play poker?" I said.

She looked at me like I was a talking turnip.

By the time she was finished with stuffing and

beautifying herself, it was midnight. She didn't like any of our DVDs, so we turned on the TV and watched everything I hated. We were sitting up in my bed in our pj's. Hers were dark-purple with light-purple dots. She ate a whole bag of Reese's Mini Pieces and never offered me one. I made the big mistake of going to the bathroom. When I got back she was sprawled on her stomach in the middle of the bed, sleeping. I stood over her, studying the situation. I whispered, "Anna." No answer. I gave her a little nudge. "Unnnh unnnh," she went, and flapped her hand at me like I was a moth. I gave up. I grabbed a blanket from the hall closet and slept on the floor.

At breakfast my mother greeted her with a big smile and even a hug and said, "Okay, Anna, what'll it be? Cereal? Eggs? Pancakes?"

"French toast," she said.

She ordered five slices of French toast and ate two. She wanted blueberry syrup, but all we had was maple. She kept saying, "Boy, this would *really* be good with blueberry syrup."

I was terrified she would hang around all day. And then I got lucky. Halfway through breakfast,

I let out a burp. I didn't even mean it. It was an accident. It was also a doozie, a world-class ripper, one of my best ever. If you're wondering about my parents, they don't even bother to yell, "Lily!" anymore, except when there's company. So I guess my mother figured she had to do something, so she says, "Lily," and gives me a halfhearted glare. As for the overnight guest—ha!—she practically choked on her mouthful. Her eyes went wide and her face twisted like some chain-saw killer was loose in the kitchen. (Other kids just laugh and tell me to do it again.) I patted my chest. "Great French toast, huh?" I said. She took off right after breakfast. I carried her purple suitcase halfway down the block.

Later that day I told Poppy, "Now I feel worse than ever. And I hate my favorite color."

Poppy acted like it was no big deal. "Hey—win some, lose some."

"But it just shows you how rotten my life is now," I told him. "I was *born* with a built-in sleepover person. It was perfect. Why did it all have to change?"

"That's life," he said. "Change. If you're smart

you'll change with it. Took me a long time to learn that."

"If change means Anna Matuzak," I said, "I'll *never* change."

He laughed. "There's other ways. And one thing hasn't changed—Anna or no Anna, you still need a life."

So we thought about it, or rather Poppy thought about it. I have no idea how to think about getting a life.

"Hobby," he said. "You need a hobby."

"I have one," I told him. "Trains. You know that."

"That's more of an interest than a hobby," he said. "And anyway, trains obviously are not doing the trick. You need something that will occupy a lot of your time. Hours a day."

"Like what?" I said.

"Like . . . stamp collecting."

"Stamp collecting?" I wanted to barf. "Oh, pul-eeeeeze."

Jake

So he painted his clubhouse yellow.

And next day there it was again, splashed across the side. In black. Nice contrast with the yellow.

SOOP

Of course this time it was no surprise to us. Bump had told us he was going to do it.

"Who do you think's doing it?" Soop said as we pulled up to the curb.

"Doing what?" said Bump, all innocent, like before.

"Painting my name on the clubhouse," said Soop.

"Oh, that," said Nacho.

Bump leaned in and whispered to me, "Listen to him. *Look* at him."

I knew what Bump meant. The goober still wasn't mad, just curious, like this was a math problem he hadn't run into before. He should have been pulling out his hair, howling, *What's going on?*, maybe even crying. But all he did was talk all calm with his hands on his hips, like he owned the world. That's what gets you. You know if it happened to you, you'd be going nuts, you'd want to kill somebody. And then you see this kid who refuses—flat-out *refuses*—to be normal. Who stands there with his hands on his hips, all cocky-like. And if there's one thing that burns your butt more than anything else, it's a cocky goober. So naturally you want to smack him, slap some normal into him.

But Bump stays cool. "I don't know," he says. "Who do *you* think's doing it, Erno?"

"Beats me," said Soop. "It's a mystery."

We all nodded: "Mystery . . ."

And now Soop was giggling. Another thing that drives the ice pick into your neck: a giggling goober.

"What's so funny, Erno?" said Bump.

"He *still* can't spell *soup*!" goes Erno. He went on giggling, like it was the funniest thing since cow pies.

His hand shot into the air. "Hold the presses!" He turned to us—"Wait here, guys"—and sprinted into his house. He was back in a couple minutes with a little paint can and a thin brush. He went to the wall. "I couldn't find any black," he called. He painted blue happy faces into the double *O*s. He turned to us. He threw out his arms. "Ta-da!"

Bump started a slow handclap that of course Soop didn't realize was bogus. The rest of us joined in. Bump hissed, almost loud enough for Soop to hear, "This is his last day as a happy goober."

Lily

I caved in. I'll try stamp collecting.

Jake

We could see it a mile away. It's probably visible from the space station. We were laughing so hard we were wobbling as we rode down the street. Nacho crashed into a curb.

The paint job looked like the head-on wreck of two rainbows. I never saw so many colors in one place, all splashed and squished and slopped all over each other.

And there was the supergoober, ducking through the doorway and coming out to greet us— laughing. I swear, he was laughing even harder than us. And the more he laughed, the less Bump laughed. And when Soop threw out his arms and yelled, "It's *beautiful*!" I think I saw steam coming off the top of Bump's head.

Lily

Stamp collecting lasted a day.

I'm trying homemade greeting cards.

Jake

Today it was a missing board. Halfway up the side facing the street.

We were staring at it for a while when suddenly Soop's face appeared in the gap.

"Hi, guys!" he called, all cheery. "Look—somebody gave me a window!"

Bump's tires bit the asphalt as he peeled out.

Lily

Scratch homemade greeting cards.
I'll try reading palms.

Jake

Just me, Nacho, and Burke at the hideout today. Bump is away on vacation with his family. But his calling cards were all around us—black clumps of chewed-up licorice. He doesn't eat his licorice all the way anymore. He folds a couple sticks in his cheek and chews and sucks and then spits out the wad. I think he thinks he's chewing tobacco.

So we didn't ride over to Soop's. It's not the same without Bump. He always does most of the talking. But there was still plenty to hee-haw about—for the first time we weren't just laughing about Soop. We were laughing about Bump too. About how he was getting madder and madder each day.

"Did you see him the other day? Did he blast

outta there or what?" said Burke.

"I saw snots shooting out his ears!" said Nacho.

That's how it went. Hey, we understood. Nothing is more maddening than a goober who won't get mad. It's like they cheat you out of your fun. It's like you throw a dart at a goober and all he does is say, "That tickles," and throws it back at you, feather first. If you can't have fun with a goober, what's the point? So yeah, we saw Bump's problem. We sympathized with him. But that didn't make it any less funny.

Before we left the hideout, Nacho got a stick and scratched in the dirt:

SUPERGOOBER 10
BUMP 0

And we laughed harder than ever.

Lily

I read Poppy's palm. I told him he's going to buy me a car on the day I turn sixteen. He pulled his hand away. "That's it for your palm-reading career."

Jake

We've just been goofing off the last couple days. Riding around. Playing a little basketball. Skipping stones at the creek. We even did little-kid stuff at the park. Swings. Seesaw. At one point I found myself standing at the bottom of the sliding-board ladder. I was third in line, staring down at the head tops of two little preschool runts. That's how bad summer can get. You wonder why you were so thrilled back on the first day.

"Bor-ing," said Burke.

"That's the last sliding-board line I'll ever stand in in my life, if I live to be a thousand," I said.

"I miss Bump," said Burke.

"I miss Soop," said Nacho.

"You know what we are?" I said.

"What?" said Nacho.

"Goober addicts."

Lily

"How about origami?" said Poppy.

"What's origami?"

"Folding paper. You make things—birds, boats, almost anything. I saw kids doing it all over Japan."

"I make great paper airplanes," I said.

We went to the library for a book on origami.

Jake

So without Bump, we rode over to Soop's. He wasn't there working on the shack. We were surprised, but maybe we shouldn't have been. We usually ride over in the morning, but this was afternoon.

We were ready to push off when we heard a voice calling, "Hi boys!" At first we didn't know where it was coming from. Then we saw a face sticking out of a second-floor window. A lady. Had to be his mother. "Hold on there a minute, boys," she said. "I'll be right down."

"Uh-oh," said Burke. "She knows."

"Knows what?" I said.

"Who's been messing up the shack," said Burke.

"Yeah—Bump," said Nacho. "We're in the clear."

"I don't feel in the clear," I said.

And then there she was, bouncing out the front door and across the porch and down the steps. She charged straight for us like a fullback. I wished we had cleared out. Her arm was coming up. I got ready to duck. I started to say, "Bump—" I never got to say *did it* because a massive grin broke across her face, and that was no fist on the end of her arm but a hand to shake. "You must be—let me guess—Jake?" She acted all proud of herself when I grunted and shook her hand. She got Burke and Nacho right too. She laughed out loud. "Nacho—I *love* it! Always wished I had a cool nickname." She stepped back. "I'm Heather. Ernie's mom."

My memory is kind of fuzzy on some of this. Probably because it was one of the uncomfortablest times of my life. I mean, everybody knows how to deal with a goober. But how about a goober's *mom*? There's no manual for that.

Mrs. Goober took another step back, as if to get us all in the picture. "So," she said, and just grinned away. *Here it comes*, I thought: *So you're the hoodlums that have been terrorizing my son.* She had short curly brown hair. And hoop earrings you could spit through. And a T-shirt that said I BRAKE

FOR TURTLES. At last she went on, "Finally I get to meet you. I see you coming by all the time, talking to Ernie. Sometimes I've been tempted to come out and say hello, but I see you guys laughing and having a good time and I say, 'Nah, stay outta their business.' Was I right, guys?"

We glanced at each other. How are you supposed to answer that?

She laughed. "I retract the question." She looked back over her shoulder at the paint-splashed, lopsided shack. "She's a beauty, huh?"

Burke and I just nodded, but Nacho piped, "Absolutely."

She shot a look at Nacho and her cheeks bulged and her lips quivered and a laugh just barfed out, she couldn't hold it in, and I knew that in her howling laughter she was telling us that she knew that we knew it was the most ridiculous-looking building in the history of mankind. She wiped her eyes. "Well, Wednesday is your pal Ernie's art lesson day, so I guess you're stuck with me." She looked us over again, giving us a grin that seemed like a secret behind a zipper. "I know, I know, you just want to get outta here, escape the old lady."

She gave a big dramatic shrug. "Sorry, guys." She waved and headed for the house. "Come on in." We stayed. She turned. The grin was gone. "I *said* come in." We parked our bikes and followed her into the house.

She led us to the kitchen. She gave us lemonade to drink. ("We don't believe in soda, dudes.") And food. Oatmeal cookies. Brownies. Carrot sticks. Onion dip. Blue corn chips. ("Sorry, no nachos, Nacho." She giggled for a whole minute over that one.)

She asked a lot of questions. She wanted to know everything about us, like she was writing a book or something. I don't mean she was grilling us. It was all friendly. She seemed so interested, nodding her head and saying, "Really?" and "Is that so?" The more she nodded, the more we talked. I found out stuff about Nacho and Burke I never knew. And when Burke pointed to me and said, "He's a twin," and Nacho said, "His twin is a sister," she went bonkers.

"Wow—Jake—no kidding? I always thought it would be *so* cool to have a twin. What's it like?" Before I could answer, she said, "Never mind. Dumb question. Way too broad. Okay—what's her name?"

"Whose name?" I said.

That really cracked her up. I think she thought I was trying to be a comic. "Your *twin sister*," she said.

"Lily," I said.

"Lily." She smiled. She repeated it, like she was tasting it. "Lily." The smile got dreamy. "Jake and Lily." She took awhile to digest that, then: "Okay . . . so . . . tell me, is it true about twins, like, you almost *know* what each other is thinking? Stuff like that?"

Suddenly everybody was looking at me. What could I say? How could I put into words for her something that we could never put into words for ourselves? Unless you count *goombla*. But more than that, her question smacked me up against something that's been there for a while, I guess, I just never really looked—*it's not that way anymore*. I suddenly realized how long it's been since I knew what my sister's been writing in her journal chapters. I remembered the fights with her, trying to tell her to chill out, we're just growing up, that's all.

Mrs. G was tilting, smiling at me. She laid her

hand on mine. "Forget it, Jake. Some things just can't be put into words, right?"

I looked at her. Something inside me said, *Thank you*. I nodded.

She took it easy on me from then on, and it was pretty okay. I kept thinking, *I'm in a supergoober's house!* But when I looked around the place, it looked like mine. Somewhere along the line it occurred to me that I wasn't uncomfortable anymore. At the last second, as we walked out the door, I remembered to say, "Thank you." Then the other guys did too. She stood at the door. She waved at us as we pedaled off.

We didn't go back to the hideout. We didn't talk. We just rode around. From one end of town to the other and back. I know we were all thinking it, but nobody was saying it. Finally Nacho did: "First goober mother I ever met."

"She's pretty cool," I said.

"She called us dudes," said Burke.

We rode some more, then split and went home to our dinners.

Lily

I stink at origami. Whatever I tried to make came out looking like a giraffe in a bathtub.

Poppy thought about it. He snapped his fingers. "How about this: flowers. You like flowers, don't you?"

"I don't know," I said. "I don't think about them."

"Everybody likes flowers," he said. "You're gonna help me landscape the backyard. Come on."

So we went to a garden shop and came back with a bunch of plants and flowers and a pair of trowels. He told me maybe I'm a green thumb and just don't know it.

"What's a green thumb?" I said. I looked at my thumb.

"Somebody who's good with plants," he said. "Green thumbs can make anything grow."

As soon as we went out the back door I knew I was in trouble. A dog was barking. It was in the next-door backyard. A big black dog. Sticking its nose through one of the diamond-shaped spaces in the chain-link fence and barking. I don't mean a nice regular doggie *woof woof* bark. I mean a loud, nasty, growly bark. The kind of bark that's so powerful it makes the dog's head flop up and down. A bark that's super excited, but not in a puppy-happy-to-see-you way. Super excited because he can't wait to sink his teeth into you and rip out a vital organ.

"No way," I said. I stepped back behind the screen door.

My grandfather laughed. "He just barks. He's a big baby. Look." He went to the fence. The dog went even crazier. "Poppy!" I yelled, but Poppy was reaching over the fence and noogling the black ears, and the beast was licking his hand.

"It's me," I called. "Dogs hate me. They know I'm scared."

Poppy came back and took my hand. He didn't try to drag me out. He would never force me. He just said, quiet and smiling and looking into my eyes, "You're safe with me, Lil."

I hate to say this, but I didn't totally believe it. I went with him because I could see that he believed it, and I didn't want to hurt his feelings. "I'll work over here," I said, and headed for the side of the yard away from the dog. Poppy laughed, and we spent the next hour digging holes and planting stuff and watering with the hose. The dog stared at us for a while, then went sniffing around its own yard. I have to admit we never heard another peep out of it. I don't care. I told Poppy that as long as that beast is next door, my new life isn't going to be happening in his backyard.

Jake

When we showed up at the hideout this morning, the first thing we noticed was the dirt. The Bump vs Supergoober score was gone. Scuffed away totally.

"Looks like Bump's back from vacation," said Nacho.

Burke pointed his sneaker toe at a couple of heel holes. "I guess he didn't think our little joke was too funny."

We rode past his house. We didn't see him. We hung out front for a little while, staring at the windows. No sign of anybody.

"Maybe he's not back from vacation," I said. "Maybe somebody else scratched it out."

Burke sneered. "Yeah, right."

"Maybe he's in there," said Nacho. "All we gotta do is knock."

But nobody did.

We rode off. Nobody said, "Let's go to Soop's," but our bikes seemed to be heading there anyway. We were still a couple blocks away when Burke suddenly said, "Stop."

Burke has the best eyes, but it didn't take long for me and Nacho to catch up. The shack, visible from outer space, was gone. Well, not completely gone. It was now in a pile. A jagged splashy pile of colors. Like pick-up sticks.

"Holy crap," said Burke.

Lily

Poppy is better at getting a life than I am. He just got a job. Part-time. Mornings. At the rec center. Watching preschool kids. I thought only ladies did that stuff.

He gave me a key to the house so I can still go over in the mornings when I want.

I sat in the house alone today. In the new easy chair. The new TV was right in front of me but I didn't turn it on. I stared at the deck of cards in the middle of the table. I was feeling lonely, but not because I was alone. I feel lonely even when there's people around.

When Poppy came home from work we had lunch together. Then we played poker. Long ago I cleaned him out of beetles. Now our money is pistachio nuts. He lets me cheat all I want, but it's hardly fun anymore. It's getting harder and harder for even Poppy to make me happy. As much as I love my grandpa, he can't replace my twin brother.

Things that never used to be questions are questions now.

What is Jake doing?

What's he thinking?

How is he feeling?

What's he writing in the journal today?

The answers keep hitting me like a smack in the face.

I don't know!

I don't know!

I'm dreading our birthday. It's coming up soon. I'm scared it's going to be different. I'm scared we won't meet at the train station that night. That's going to be the test. That's going to be the final answer. I know it and I'm terrified it's going to be the wrong answer. Because in spite of everything that's happened, in spite of the way I talk and the way I feel, there's still a little crumb of hope somewhere inside me. A little crumb that whispers: *Hey, if he shows up at the station, then you're still cool, it's not so bad after all*. But if he doesn't show up, it will mean our goombla is gone. Totally. *Fssst*. It will mean I'm right. But I don't want to be right. I want to be wrong. I'm terrified.

And I'm lost.

For the first time in my life I feel lost. I wasn't lost that day at the beach. Not this Neverlost Twin. Last year you could have dropped me in the middle of the Amazon jungle and I wouldn't have been lost. But I am now.

I'm lonely and I'm scared and I'm lost.

Jake

Eyes open, eyes shut, makes no difference. I keep seeing it. Pick-up sticks.

Lily

I went up to the Cool-It Room, where I had once
been so happy. Joe the gorilla sat on the rocking chair, still grinning at me. I walked around,
touched things, remembered. The Monopoly board
was on the floor, stopped in the middle of a game
we never finished. Jake's top hat was sitting on
Boardwalk. So were red hotels. I guess he was winning. Most of all it was the walls that got to me.
Two of them, from the floor to as high as two little
kids could reach, were filled with tic-tac-toe games.
I cried. I got my pillow and my stuffed watermelon
and a blanket to lie on. I'll sleep here tonight.

Jake

Is it *our* fault? Leaving that 10–0 score in the dirt for Bump to see? Did *that* push him over the edge? What did we think? Did we think Bump was just going to laugh it off? *Bump Stubbins?* Who said, "He's gonna pay"? Who said, "This is his last day as a happy goober"? *That* Bump Stubbins?

SOOP in giant letters. The paint jobs. The ripped-out plank. And what did all that do to the goober? Absolutely nothing. The more Bump did, the more Soop laughed, and the more Soop laughed, the madder Bump got. And then he comes home from vacation and sees the score in the dirt in the hide-out. What did we expect? Why are we surprised? Which brings me back to the beginning: is it *our* fault?

Lily

In the Cool-It Room last night, in the dark, I heard a train whistle. So sad and faraway. Like it was lost, calling for its mate. . . . *Where are you? . . . Where are you? . . . Wait for me. . . .*

Jake

It feels like I should go over there. But why? What would I say? To him? To his mother? She was nice to us. To me especially. Her name is Heather.

But I'm not going over.

Lily

One more day till July 29. The Big B. I'll be at the station. He won't. One more day till the end of my life as I know it.

Jake

Ernie. Heather. That's all. We don't even know their last name.

I was thinking this when the guys showed up on my porch this morning. Including Bump. "Let's go, Jake-o," he said. He seemed like his old self, the same old bold boss of the Death Rays. He held a fist high. He fired a howitzer of black licorice spit. "I'm back and I'm ready to *rrrrumble*!" No sign that he even knew about the situation. I couldn't help thinking, *Maybe he didn't do it after all.* Burke and Nacho were staring off into space.

I didn't even have time to wish we weren't heading for Meeker Street because that's exactly where Bump led us. *Okay*, I thought, *at least have it be cleared away by now. Just an empty yard.* No luck.

From a couple blocks away I could see not a thing had changed. The bright rubble of colors. Pick-up sticks.

"Hey—what happened?" said Bump.

Nobody said anything. Nobody knew exactly what game we were playing. Was Bump acting? Was he innocent?

Bump hit the brakes. He said it again. "What happened?" It was obvious we weren't going another inch till he got an answer. He was looking at me.

"Looks like somebody trashed the shack," I garfed out.

Bump gazed down the street. His eyes, his voice got all wondery: "Wow . . . really?"

"Yeah," I said.

"Who did it?" he said.

Maybe the same person who did the paint job and tore out the plank, I thought. "Beats me," I said.

He blinked. Some of the most innocent blinks I ever saw. He leaned into a pedal. "Let's go see," he said.

We pulled up to the curb. No sign of anyone.

"Nobody home," said Nacho. "Let's motor."

"Wait a sec," said Bump. "Wait a sec." He

leaned on his handlebars, staring at the heap. The only thing I could read on his face was curiosity. As I was praying, *Please don't let her be looking out the window,* the back screen door creaked and Soop came out. And in that split instant I knew: *goobers are* not *invincible.*

For the first time ever he was not smiling. He was not waving *hi, guys!* He wasn't even wearing his orange hat. He came to us. He looked in our eyes. "See what somebody did," he said.

In his face I saw massive sadness. And yet there wasn't a clue of a tear on his cheek, not a quiver on his lip. *Goobers are brave,* I thought.

"Wow," said Bump, wagging his head. "And it was such an awesome clubhouse too. What're you gonna do now?"

Soop didn't hesitate. "Rebuild."

Bump scoffed. "Rebuild? That's dumb. They'll just do it again. You should go find who did it and beat him up." He said this with a totally straight face.

"I don't beat up people," said Soop.

Bump boggled. *"Really?* You *don't*? Not *ever*?"

"Not ever," said Soop, all serious, as if he *could*

beat up somebody if he wanted to. His arms were the size of straws (like mine). And of course, goobers don't fight anyway.

"Well, maybe you should," said Bump, whose body is the opposite of Soop's, thick and chesty. "Catch that guy and teach him a lesson."

I noticed that Soop was no longer paying attention to Bump. He was staring at the heap. When he turned back to us, his eyes were glittery. *"Why?"* he said.

This took Bump by surprise. "Huh?"

"Why?" said Soop.

"Why what?" said Bump.

"Why would somebody do this?"

The worst part about the question was that he was looking at all of us, asking us all. The answer finally came from Bump, and it practically blew me off my bike. "Maybe because somebody can't stand goobers."

The world stopped. Soop's eyes were big as bike tires. You could see them coming into focus. He blinked. "Bump?" He pointed. *"You."* His voice was flat and hard as a two-by-four. *"You* did it."

"Ha!" Bump laughed. Then his face went

blank. "No I didn't."

"Yes," said Soop. "You did." He took a step forward. I was amazed. This was not the Soop I knew.

Bump rolled his bike into the curb. They were inches apart. "You calling me a liar—*Soop*?"

Soop nodded, all serious, as if he were answering a question in class. "Yes."

Bump opened his mouth and let his licorice wad drop onto Soop's sneaker. While Soop was looking down at the sneaker, Bump sucker-shoved him. Shoved him hard. Soop went lurching backward, skinny arms windmilling. He landed on his butt halfway into the yard. He popped up and came charging, fury in his eyes, his hands balled into bony little fists. He was screaming. Just before he got to Bump, I threw out my hands. "Stop!" I yelled. "*I* did it!"

Lily

Last night I had a dream. I was falling. I wasn't scared. But I had two other feelings. Surprise and disappointment. Because I expected somebody to catch me and it wasn't happening. So I kept falling.

Tonight is the night. I'm afraid to go to sleep.

Jake

Why did I do it?

As he was landing on his butt, popping up and charging, there wasn't a thought in my head. It's like I was somebody else. Somebody else's arms were pushing out and somebody else's voice was yelling, "Stop! *I* did it!"

The best answer I can come up with is that I must have taken pity on him because he was about to get destroyed. Maybe I figured the only way to save the stupid goober from himself was to take the heat off Bump. But really, what would Bump have done? He'd have bopped the goober once in the nose, and the goober would have gone crying and running into the house and we'd never ride back to Meeker Street again and that would be that.

So if I had it to do over, would I?

No way.

Because the worst that would have happened would have been one bloody nose. And that would have been cheap compared to the price I started to pay as soon as I said those words.

I'll never forget that face. It turned from Bump to me. What I remember most is how slow it turned. And then the eyes. The fury drained out of them. What took its place was something I hope I never have to see again. It was shock. Pure shock. It came with a terrible one-word question: *"Jake?"* That word, that look punched a hole right through me. At that moment I hated my own name. And since he said it with a question mark, I guess that was my test, my chance to laugh and say, "Just kidding—you're right, it was Bump." But time ran out—*pencils up!*—and the shock on his face was changing to something even worse: hurt. I've seen hurt before—who hasn't?—but this was a whole other kind of hurt. This was somebody else's hurt aimed at *me*.

No other words were said. The Death Rays were just gawking at me, like *huh?* As for the kid, he just seemed to slump away to nothingness. I mean, it wasn't just a shoulder slump. His whole body slumped. In fact, if he had a glass chest I think I would have seen his heart and his lungs and his kidneys slumping too. Pretty soon nothing was left but those eyes. *Stop looking at me like that!* I wanted to scream. And then he turned and went into the house, and we rode away.

The only one who asked me about it was Nacho: "Why'd you do it, man?" I just shrugged. Nobody mentioned it again.

Lily

I woke up at the train station. But that was all. No blinding-light, train-through-me dream. No smell of pickles. No Jake.

Like always, I was in my pajamas. The cement platform was cool under my bare feet.

The platform and the tracks were lit from high lamps above both ends of the station. The shadow of the roof edge split the platform into day and night. I could hardly see the benches. The station windows were black. I squinted into the shadows. I whispered, "Jake? . . . You there?"

I went to the edge of the platform. The night swallowed up the tracks, left and right. My toes hung over the cool, hard edge. "Jake!" I yelled. "Jake!"

I don't know how long I stood there. I kept thinking, *Maybe he's just late.*

I heard something behind me. I turned. The station door was opening. A shadow moving through the shadows.

"Jake?" I said.

The shadow spoke. "The things I do for my grandkids."

Poppy?

He came into the light. He was groggy, slumpy. He looked at his watch. He mumbled something. I think it was, "Three o'clock . . ." The only awake part of him was his eyes. They stared at me. He reached out and poked me in the shoulder. Twice.

What was going on? I was getting worried. "Poppy," I said, "why are you here? Did something bad happen?"

"You could say that," he mumbled. "I fell asleep." He looked around. "He's not here?"

"No," I said.

He looked down at me. "No." He palmed the top of my head. "Sorry, kid."

"Poppy," I screeched, "why are *you* here?"

He took a deep breath. "In case this was going

to happen, I thought somebody oughta be here. You shouldn't be alone." He looked around again. He looked at his watch again. "Maybe he's just late."

I screamed, "There is no late!" I lost it. "My life is over!" I wailed. I crumpled to the ground.

He picked me up. I'm too old to be carried now, but I didn't fight it. He took me to his bike. He helped seat me on the bar in front of him and pedaled off. He grumbled: "Gotta get a car." The last thing I remember is clinging like an octopus to him as he lugged me up the stairs to my bedroom. I had the falling dream again. Nobody was catching me.

Jake

I must have been grogging around my room for a couple minutes before I saw the sign. It was Scotch-taped on the closed door. Mom does it every year. Now that my sister and I have our own rooms, I guess she did one for each of us. Homemade. White paper. Red letters sprinkled with glitter:

Happy Birthday

That's when it hit me: *I just woke up in my bed—not the train station!*

I wasn't sure how I felt about that. I wondered if my sister was there. Maybe she wasn't. Maybe she's outgrowing that magical twin stuff too. Maybe it was nothing more than that favorite word of grown-ups: a phase.

No party this year. Just family, which now includes Poppy. Of course Dad had to set up the stepladder in the driveway and plant the adorable twins next to it and take our picture to show how we're growing up the ladder year by year.

"You're way past the fourth rung now," said Dad.

"Heading for the top," said Mom.

"Need a bigger ladder soon," said Poppy.

My best present was five stones from Poppy. He collected them in his travels, just for me.

Lily got a Gray Shadow Crimestoppers kit. She didn't exactly look thrilled. She slept till noon. We were supposed to go to the water park, but we didn't because she said her stomach hurt. She didn't say a word to me all day.

Whatever. I have my own problems. How was I supposed to enjoy my birthday when all I could see was Ernie's eyes? Those grown-ups grinning at me—I wanted to say, *You wouldn't be grinning if you knew what a rat I am.*

In my room at night a question came in the dark: *Why do you even* care *what a goober thinks about you?*

There was no answer.

Lily

I haven't written in this journal for a week. I'm too depressed to do anything. I don't go to Poppy's. I don't want to be around anybody I know. I ride my bike. I wander the mall.

My birthday was Crap City. I got the Gray Shadow Crimestoppers kit. It has a hat and magnifying glass and handcuffs and whistle and Crimestoppers manual, and I couldn't care less. I just wanted the day to be over. Poppy whispered that he was never so nervous in his life as he was sneaking me back into my room. If I thought my parents wouldn't make me get up, I'd still be in bed.

Jake

I can't sleep. Those eyes hang over me in the dark, like burning stones. Eyes might not speak louder than mouths, but they speak deeper, the terrible name: *Jake? Jake?*

We meet in the hideout. We get takeout and eat lunch there. We ride. We hang. We goof off. We spit-bomb cars from the bridge. We still laugh, but not as much as before. Sometimes I wonder if the others can see those eyes following me. My pumpkin seeds don't taste so good anymore.

Lily

My first thought was: *I don't believe Mom is dragging me out of bed so early. It's summer freaking vacation!* Then I opened my eyes. It wasn't Mom. It was Poppy. "Let's go," he said. He tickled my feet. I shrieked. "You've been a zombie long enough. I'm off work today. You're spending it with me."

We went to used car lots, and by noon we were riding home in an old Malibu.

"Wish it wasn't red," he said. "But the price was right."

"Red's okay," I told him.

After lunch we went for a spin. Back home, he went for the cards. "Ready to lose millions?" he said.

"Nah," I said. "Don't feel like it."

He snapped his fingers. "Bummer. I guess my strategy's not working. I figured if I kept you busy all day, maybe I could drag you out of your mood."

We were at the kitchen table, our usual card-playing place. "I'll never be out of this mood," I said. I slumped in my chair.

"Sure you will," he said. "Bad moods don't last forever."

"It's not even just a mood," I told him. "It's my life. It's me. You don't understand."

He shuffled the cards over and over. "I understand time passes. Time heals."

I stared at him. "Poppy, you're not a twin. You don't know what it's like to lose half of your self."

He stared back at me for a long time. His eyes were shining. He smiled—a sad, remembering smile. He nodded. "Oh yes I do."

It took me another minute of staring, and then I got it. *Grandma.* I felt rotten. I reached out. "I'm sorry, Poppy. I forgot."

He patted my hand. He sniffed. "It's okay. You're allowed."

I looked at Poppy's white ponytailed hair, at

his eyes, at his face. I thought, *Wow—love lasts a long time.*

And then he was talking. About the old days in California. Him and Grandma. How they used to dig for clams on the beaches of the Pacific Ocean. How they stomped on grapes and scrubbed the purple off each other's feet and made their own wine. How sometimes Grandma would suddenly bust out laughing and he would look around but he couldn't see anything funny. "Why are you laughing?" he would ask her, and she would say, "Who needs a reason?" and pretty soon they were both doing it. "We'd look at each other and just out of the blue bust out laughing."

I watched his hands shuffle the cards. I knew he wanted me to play. I knew I should. But I couldn't.

When I looked up, the same smile was on his face, but the eyes were different. A minute ago they were reaching back across time and miles to California and Grandma. Now they were only reaching three feet—thirty-six inches—to the other side of the kitchen table. To me.

"Poppy, what?" I said.

He was wagging his head now.

"What?"

"It's not that I didn't believe you. You know . . . the sleepwalk, the train station, all that."

"Okay. So?"

"I mean, if I didn't believe you, I wouldn't have been there that night. Would I?"

It was feeling a little heavy. I tried to lighten it. "Even if you *were* a little late."

He chuckled. "Right on that. But then . . . then . . . seeing you with my own eyes, standing there on the platform in the dim light, in your bare feet and pajamas, *all by yourself*"—he wagged his head some more—"touching you—remember that?—I touched you, I *poked* you, remember?"

I nodded. I couldn't speak.

"Lily . . . I've been around the world, I've seen it all, but that night . . . you . . ."

I rushed to him. I dived into his lap. There were no more words. Just being close. And I think it was not just Poppy who was squeezing me. I think it was Grandma too.

Jake

Lindop.

That's his last name. I had to give the eyes a name. The face I dream about every night, it had to have a name. A full name.

I rode to Meeker Street. I didn't have to worry about him because today was Wednesday and that's when he goes to his art lesson. That left his mom, who actually scared me more than him. I didn't go straight to the house. I parked my bike a block away, sat on the curb, and watched. I must have waited two hours before the mailman finally came along. As soon as I saw him stick mail into the box by the front door, I took a deep breath and started walking. I wore a dorky shirt I never wear. I wore my sister's Pennsylvania Railroad hat. And sunglasses. It was the best disguise I could come up with. Every step of the way I was ready to run if I heard somebody yell, "Hey!"

I turned up the walkway to the porch. I was never so terrified in my life. I kept my head down. I prayed she wasn't looking out the second-floor window. I prayed she wouldn't come out just as I was reaching into the box. I grabbed the stack of mail. My hands were shaking. I looked at one letter. It was addressed to Mr. Raymond Lindop. Another letter. Another. Each one with the same last name: Lindop. I stuffed the mail back into the box and took off straight across the yard. Lily's hat flew off but I was too terrified to go back for it. I climbed onto my bike and flew. I was sure somebody saw me. I tried to remember if looking at somebody's mail was a crime. I didn't calm down till I was out of town.

I kept repeating it. Silently at first, then out loud:

"Lindop . . . Lindop . . . Ernest Lindop . . ."

Lily

"I was wrong."

That's what Poppy said when I walked into his kitchen tonight. He looked up from the sink and said, "I was wrong."

"About what?" I said.

He turned from the sink. He was holding a cantaloupe. He held it out to me. "What can I do with this?"

I groaned. I grabbed the cantaloupe. I slammed it on the counter. "Jeez, Poppy, don't you know *any-thing*?" I yanked open the counter drawer. All I saw were a couple of butter knives, forks, and spoons. "Where's your long knife?" I said. "For cutting big stuff?"

He looked at me like I was speaking Chinese. "Long knife?"

I glared at him. "How do you expect to cut a watermelon? Slice bread? Cake? A turkey?"

"I'll get a long knife," he said.

I stared at the pitiful drawer. I shook my head. "You're not even civilized. You don't even have an ice-cream scoop."

"I don't eat ice cream," he said.

I snapped. "Well, *I* do!"

"Okay—okay," he said. "I'll get a long knife and an ice-cream scoop."

"And fudge ripple," I told him. "Every time I come to this house, I want there to be fudge ripple ice cream in the freezer. You know what a freezer is, don't you?"

He saluted. "Yes, ma'am."

I poured myself an OJ from the fridge. "See, you got me all worked up."

"Must be Bite Off Grandpa's Head Day."

I snicker-snorted. "Sorry. I'm in a crappo mood." I flopped into a chair. "So what are you so wrong about?"

He sat down. "My advice to you. Telling you to get a life. Origami. Gardening. All that."

"Why's it wrong?"

"It's wrong because—" He stopped, stared at me. "Look—what's the bottom line here? What are we trying to accomplish?"

I didn't have to think long. "Get me back with my brother. Get our goombla back."

He smacked the table. "Exactly. And listen to the word you said—*get*."

"So?"

"So, goombla, twin magic—whatever you want to call it—it's not something you can chase after, reach for, *get*. You've been trying too hard. You're forcing it."

This time *I* smacked the table. "Well duh, of *course* I'm forcing it. I *want* it."

He shook his head. "Doesn't work that way. It's like love. You can't *try* to love somebody. Either it's there or it's not."

I felt a chill. "Are you saying our goombla isn't there? It doesn't exist? I might as well give up?"

He patted my hand. He laughed. "It's there, all

right. Once entangled, forever entangled. You have to trust that."

I was getting dizzy from all this fancy thinking. "So I just wasted the last couple of weeks—because I was trying too hard?"

He nodded. "Right."

"So what am I supposed to do now?"

He smiled. "Stop trying. Give life a chance to just happen."

"Poppy," I whined, "you're driving me crazy. First you say try. Now you say don't try. First you say get a life. Now you say don't get a life."

He nodded, like I was making perfect sense. "Right. Because *life* will get *you*. Took me awhile to figure that out."

"But what about my brother? What about us? Our goombla?"

He flicked his hand. "Walk away from it. Turn your back on it." He smiled. "Forget it."

I pounded the table. "Never!"

He took both my hands in his. "Listen, your goombla is a gift. You didn't ask for it and you can't give it away. But you're smothering it. It can't breathe. You need to back off. Let go of it."

I cried, "I can't!"

He stood. He got the cantaloupe. He sat it in the middle of the table. He patted it. "Now stand up and turn around."

"Poppy—"

"Do it. Stand up and turn your back on the cantaloupe."

I stood up. I turned around.

"Can you see it?" he said.

"No."

"Okay, now turn back."

I did.

"And what do you see on the table?"

"A cantaloupe."

"It didn't disappear when you turned your back, did it?"

"Poppy—"

"Did it?"

"No."

He patted the cantaloupe. "Think of this as your goombla. Every day from now on it's going to be right here, whether you give it attention or not."

I sighed. "I don't know, Poppy."

He came over and hugged me. "You don't have to know. That's what grandpas are for. All you have to do is trust me. Trust life to find you."

I looked up into my grandfather's eyes. "I trust you," I said. "It's life I don't trust."

Jake

Riding my bike, eating breakfast, tying my shoes, in my dreams—he's there, slumping, wonder-struck. . . . *Jake?. . . Jake?*

He hates me. Ernest Lindop of Meeker Street hates me. I've never been hated before. It's like sunburn on my heart.

Lily

I'm trying. I mean, I'm trying not to try.

As I was leaving Poppy's yesterday, I said, "What exactly does that mean, let go of it?"

"Erase it from your mind," he said. "Don't think about goombla. Don't care about it."

How do you not try to get something you want?

How do you stop caring about the thing that you care about the most?

How do you erase the other half of your own self?

Jake

I was wrong. Ernest Lindop doesn't hate me.

He's disappointed.

That's what it is. Disappointment. Not hate. I wish it *was* hate. Hate is easier.

It sounds pretty innocent, doesn't it? You hear parents say it all the time. Teachers. "I'm disappointed in you."

That's nothing. When somebody who was always laughing suddenly stops—when you look in a kid's eyes just at the moment when it hits him that you haven't been his friend after all—when you see somebody so sad that you know a hundred sucker punches to the gut couldn't hurt him as much as the words you just said—*that's* disappointment.

Lily

What do you do while you're waiting for your life to happen?

Do like everybody else, you could say—hang out with your best friend.

I can't. My best friend is my twin brother. Jake. The thing with best-friend-hanging is, it goes both ways. And I'm not Jake's best friend anymore.

So find another one, you could say.

Easier said than done, I say. Sure, I have friends. But mostly they're in-school friends. I've always spent most of my out-of-school time with Jake. I never had to go looking for some buddy-pal to sleep over with. I already slept over with my best friend. Every night. And now, after the Anna Matuzak Disaster, I'm practically afraid to *look* at another girl.

So that leaves Poppy. And I can only see him at night now, because he went and made them love him so much at the rec center that they made his job full-time.

So what do I do all day? Can you spell B-O-R-I-N-G?

I watch TV. I wish *The Gray Shadow* was on ten times a day.

I throw darts.

I practice burping.

I look for my missing Pennsylvania Railroad hat.

I walk along the creek and pick up cool stones that Jake would like. Then I remember Poppy's words: *Forget it.* I throw the stones into the water.

I ride my bike, looking for crimes. My Crimestoppers manual says it's not a good idea to try to make a citizen's arrest, but there's no law against it. So I take along the handcuffs, just in case I come across a crime in progress. No luck so far.

I go to Poppy's, but I stay out of the kitchen. I'm afraid to look at the table. I'm afraid the cantaloupe won't be there.

Jake

My brain is squeezing me in the middle.

The Bright Side says, *Stop blaming yourself. Day after day all you did was hang around while Bump did the talking and the mocking. You didn't paint the shack. You didn't rip off the plank. You didn't demolish the place. You didn't even come up with the name Soop. It was all Bump. All you did was step up and take the heat for him. You're not a rat. You're a hero.*

The Dark Side says, *Don't kid yourself. You're a rat. Sure, Bump carried the ball. But you were on the team. You were there the whole time, grinning and nodding and going along with the program, like Bump's little dog. Did you ever raise a finger to stop it?*

Did you ever once give the goober a break? You want proof that you're guilty? You feel guilty. Deep down you know it. You know the guilt isn't just Bump's. It's yours too. That's why you confessed.

Lily

I figured maybe I'm riding my bike too much looking for crimes. I figured it might be easier for my life to find me if I stayed put. So this morning I never left the porch. I rocked on the rocking chair.

I saw everything. The old lady across the street sweeping her driveway. Cars going by. People walking. Cats. Squirrels.

Nothing exciting. Nothing that would let me know that my new life showed up.

No crimes. Well, not officially. There was one thing that I personally would call a crime if I was a judge. It was a girl and a little kid. Her brother, I guess. The girl was pulling the kid along in a red wagon. The little kid was yelling, "Take me now!" The girl was yelling, "No!"

"Take me now!"

"No!"

That's how they went past my house:

"Now!"

"No!"

The girl looked my age. She wore a blue-and-yellow baseball cap. I didn't know her. Every time the runt said "Now!" he thumped the wagon with his feet. I felt like putting the cuffs on his feet. I could still hear them a block away:

"Now!"

"No!"

That was the big event of my fascinating day.

Jake

I don't get it. People treat me like normal. Nobody calls me names. Nobody spits on me. My mother kisses me every night when I go to bed. Don't they know I'm The Big Disappointment?

Lily

It happened again today: the girl, the runt, the wagon.

"Take me now!"

"No!"

"Now!"

"No!"

Thump. Thump.

I yelled from the rocking chair, "Shut up!"

The wagon stopped. They both turned to me, fish-eyed. Then the runt jutted out his chin and thumped the wagon. "*You* shut up!"

I didn't have any new lines, so I stuck with, "*You* shut up!"

That's how it was going—

"*You* shut up!"

"*You* shut up!"

—when I noticed the girl was marching onto my porch. I got ready in case she tried to slug me. But all she did was stick out her hand. "Thank you," she said with a big smile.

"What for?" I said.

"For telling the brat to shut up."

I shook her hand. "My pleasure."

"Do you always butt in like that?" she asked.

"Not really," I said. "It just sorta came out."

"Sydney Dodds," she said. "Two *y*'s." She stuck out her hand again.

I gave her another shake. "Lily Wambold. Two *l*'s."

"I don't know you," she said. "I live over on Clem Drive."

"I live here," I said.

She put on a mock-shock face. "Really?"

We laughed.

"So what are you doing all the way over here?" I said.

She cranked a thumb over her shoulder. "Babysitting. My summer curse. My parents both work."

"Mine too," I said. "So where does he want you to take him?"

She groaned. "McDonald's. Every day. All day long."

"He's a Big Mac freak?"

"No, he hates hamburgers. He just likes the playground."

I pictured the nearest McDonald's with one of those plastic playgrounds. "That's a couple miles away," I said.

"Exactly."

"Too far to pull a wagon."

"Will you repeat that louder, please. Devon, listen."

I called, "Too far to pull a wagon."

Devon thumped. "I wanna go!"

"Just ignore him," said Sydney.

"Tune him out."

"Exactly."

"Cool hat," I said. She wore the brim low over her eyes, like I do. It said CSX in yellow letters. "That a baseball team?"

"It's a railroad."

"Really?"

"My dad drives a freight train."

Boinnng!

I tried not to act too excited. "Cool," I said. "My brother and I were born on a train. On the California Zephyr. In the Moffat Tunnel."

"Double cool," she said. "Where's that?"

"Colorado. It's over six miles long."

"Wow. Long enough to be born." She stared at me. "You said you *and* your brother? So you're, like, *twins*?"

"Yep," I said.

"*Triple* cool."

That's what I used to think, I thought. "At least I never had to pull him around in a wagon," I said.

As we were laughing, Devon came stomping up the porch steps. He punched his sister in the leg. "I want attention!"

He was so funny with his little fist and pouty puss, we laughed even harder. So he came over and punched me. So I grabbed him and dumped him on his back and gave him the Torture of Big Girl Kisses. I stopped just short of agonizing death, and a minute later he was sitting on my lap, pulling my mouth into funny faces.

Sydney sat in the other rocker. We rocked and talked.

I got Devon my old Legos. That kept him busy on the porch floor.

I made lunch for the three of us. Tuna salad sandwiches for Sydney and me. Peanut butter and marshmallow (ugh!) for the kid.

We talked and talked. Sydney goes to Saint Catherine's. She told me all about life there. She rides her bike a lot when she's not pulling the wagon. Her father says if he can get permission, he'll take her for a ride in his engine for her next birthday. She says maybe I could come too!

I set up the croquet game in the backyard and we did that for a while. I gave Devon my stuffed watermelon to play with.

We talked.

I gave them a tour of the house. Sydney loved the basement, which is mostly my mom and dad's workshop. They make stuff for their jobs and for us. "It's like a factory!" said Sydney.

Did I say we talked?

That's what we were doing when my parents' truck pulled into the driveway. Sydney looked at her watch. "Ohmygod—I gotta get home."

I introduced her and Devon to my parents. Devon yanked my finger. "Lil-wee"—that's what he calls me—"*you* pull me home." So I walked them home, me pulling.

When we got there, Sydney was about to introduce me to her parents when Devon punched her. "Let *me* do it," he growled. He raised my hand like a winning boxer. "Mommy and Daddy—this is Lil-wee!"

I ran all the way home. I gobbled down my dinner. I biked over to Poppy's. I burst into the house. "Poppy!" I shouted. "I think my new life just found me!"

Jake

I walk the creek for stones.

I poke crayfish.

I hunt raspberries.

I still see the guys, but not as much. The name Death Rays is starting to sound a little dumb.

When we met today at the hideout—that word is starting to sound dumb too—Bump said, "I found another one!" He sucked on his licorice wad. "Let's ride!" he goes.

Bump can be like a broom. He just sweeps you along. A minute later we were all heading for the playground at Hancock School. The goober was alone on the basketball court. He couldn't bounce the ball twice in a row without losing it. Half of his shots didn't just miss the basket—they missed the *backboard*. He wore black socks with green tennis shoes and . . . well, that was enough for me. "I gotta go home," I said. "I forgot to take out the trash." I took off before they could start asking questions. "Hey, Jake!" I heard Bump call.

I guess my bike did the thinking, because before I knew it I was cruising down Meeker Street. I stopped a block away. I parked behind a car. The rubble was gone. Ernie had the four corners staked and was starting to put up the first wall. I couldn't help smiling—it was already crooked. I saw his hammer hit, then heard it a half second later. It seemed like each hammer hit was saying something. I didn't know what. I think I stayed there a long time, watching. I think I was doing something else too. I think I was rooting.

Lily

I didn't wait for them today. I met them two blocks down the street. Devon was still whining, "Take me now!"

When he saw me coming, he hopped out of the wagon and practically tackled me. "Lil-wee! *You* take me to McDonald's."

I picked him up. "Sorry, little dude. It's too far away and I don't drive."

He punched me. "I hate you!"

"I hate you too," I told him, and gave him a big wet kiss.

He went, "Ouuu!" and scraped it off with his little fist and went running back to the wagon.

"If you take him for a week, I'll give you my supercool train hat," said Sydney.

"No thanks," I said. "One brother is enough."

Sydney had a bunch of babysitting money, so we went to the dollar store and got Tootsie Pops and temporary tattoos. "On my face!" Devon piped. Before we left the store, he had four Bullwinkle tats on his cheeks and forehead.

"Your mother's gonna kill you," I told Sydney.

She shook her head. "Uh-uh. She's so happy I take him all day, I can do anything I want."

We went to Bert's Deli and got hoagies and sodas. Then I suggested we take our lunch to 214 Monroe Drive and eat it there. That's where my parents are working. They're building an addition on a house.

So that's what we did. My parents were sitting on the back steps, just opening their lunch boxes when we arrived. By the time I sat down, Devon was rooting through my mother's lunch box. My parents laughed. Sydney was mortified. "Devon!" She slapped his hand. The stolen MoonPie he was holding fell to the ground. Devon yelled, "See what you did!"

My mom picked up the MoonPie. She broke it in two and gave half to the kid. It was almost in his mouth when Sydney grabbed his wrist. "What do you say to Mrs. Wambold?"

He glared at his sister. "I say poop-poop to you."

By the time we were all done laughing, the half MoonPie was in his stomach.

My father mussed the kid's hair. "You got a handful here, big sister."

Sydney nodded. "I'm cursed."

We were all getting down to some serious munching when Devon pulled on my father's pants leg. "Will you take me to McDonald's?"

I explained the situation. My parents tried to tell Devon nicely that they had a job to do and couldn't go driving little kids around to McDonald's playgrounds every day. When my mother saw Devon's sad-sack face, I thought she was going to start bawling herself. Then she seemed to snatch a passing thought from the air. She looked at me. "Well, Lily, you know what Dad and I always say. If you want it—"

—*make it*.

Click! A light went on.

"Make it!" I said. I turned to Sydney and said

it again: "Make it!"

She looked at me. "Huh?"

"We'll *make* a playground for him. We'll do it ourselves."

I saw the light click on in her eyes. "Hey— yeah!" She looked around. She pointed. "Like . . . there?"

She was pointing to the empty lot next door. It was like a bare lawn. No shrubs or anything. Just high grass.

"You'd have to ask the owner of the property," said my dad. "You can't just go ahead and do it without permission."

"Do you know who owns it?" I asked him.

He patted the porch step. "Right here," he said. "These people. Mr. and Mrs. Addison. They own both properties."

"Mrs. Addison is inside," said Mom. "Upstairs."

I jumped up. "Let's ask her." I hauled Sydney to her feet. I looked at my parents. "Can we ask her?"

"Sure," said Dad.

"Who's stopping you?" said Mom.

We barged into the kitchen, into the dining

room, into the living room. Devon trailed us. We stopped at the foot of the stairs. I called, "Hello? Mrs. Addison?"

She came down in bare feet, cutoff jeans, and a T-shirt that said:

STOP GLOBAL WARMING

FART IN A

FREEZER

I asked her about making a playground for my friend's brother on her next-door lot. She thought for a minute. Then she made a sad smile and said, "Sorry. I'm afraid not." Because if somebody got hurt, they could be sued, she said. Plus they were thinking of putting in a vegetable garden.

"Poop," said Devon before Sydney could clamp his mouth shut.

We slunk back to the porch. I flopped down beside my mom. "We struck out," I said.

"And she had such a cool T-shirt," said Sydney.

Jake

I watched him again today. From a safe distance. This shack is going to be even crookeder than the last one. Worse than the Leaning Tower of Pisa. I kept having an urge to go help him. When my sister and I were little, our parents gave us kid-sized tool belts and started teaching us stuff about building—what kind of nails to use, what a level is for, etc. I could easily show him what he's doing wrong. But I'm the guy who confessed to wrecking his hut. No way he'll ever let me near his house again.

It was hot. I was thirsty. But I couldn't move. It's like I was hypnotized by those hammer hits. Like a clock. Like a heartbeat. There was no stopping them. All summer long. Through all the paint mess and all the wreckage . . . *bam—bam—bam*. . . . As I sat on the curb squinting through the heat shimmer, one question came through the unstoppable hammering: *why?*

Ernest Lindop, why are you doing this?

Lily

When my parents came home after work today they seemed hyped up. They both wore big grins and they were aimed at me.

"What?" I said.

"One playground coming up," said my mom.

I shrieked. "She said okay?"

Dad said, "She said, 'Sue, schmoo. We'll get insurance.'"

"What about the vegetable garden?" I said.

"She said they'd rather grow fun than squash. She said they never had kids of their own, and so now they're going to have some—this way."

I rushed to the phone to tell Sydney.

Jake

Today I found my old little-kid tool belt in the closet. I took out the carpenter's level. It was always my favorite tool. I love getting that bubble right in the middle. Then you know—you *know*—your work is straight.

I waited till after dark. I rode. I parked. I slunk across the grass. I left the level on the ground inside the half-done Leaning Shack of Meeker Street.

Lily

We cleaned up the empty lot—me, Sydney, and Devon. Not that there was much to clean up. Devon's job was to pick up stones and paper and so forth. Mrs. Addison didn't have gloves small enough for him, so she made him use a pair of sweat socks, like mittens. She gave him a plastic bag to dump stuff in. He thought he was King of the World. While the King did his job, Sydney and I fought over the lawn mower. It's a wonder a blade of grass ever got cut. We were almost done when we heard Devon shriek. We ran. He was stiff with terror, pointing at the ground. "Snake!"

I looked. It was a snake all right, but not exactly a python. It was a garter snake like I see all the time in the woods by the creek. I never understood why people, especially girls, are so terrified of snakes. This one was less than a foot long.

I picked it up. Devon gasped. I held it out to Sydney—and a funny thing didn't happen. She didn't let out a girly scream and run. She reached out and took the snake from my hand. It squirmed like a worm as she petted its head. Then she lobbed it into the Addisons' backyard. I stared at her. She gave me a smug grin. We tapped fists. She burped. I back-burped her.

I'm liking this girl more every day.

Jake

Gulp.

I used to think it was just a movie thing. Or a thing people do in stories that you read. Somebody gets nervous and surprised by a question and they can't talk, all they can do is . . . *gulp*.

But it's not just a movie thing. It's real.

Okay, back up. . . .

This morning Mom asked me to go to the super-market for two packs of kiwi fruits, which she needs for a salad tonight. I had just gotten the kiwis and was heading for the checkout when it happened. Somebody whips around with two handfuls of lettuce and bumps right into me, and while I'm staring at the lettuce, the misty thing that keeps the veggies fresh decides to go off and we're standing so close to it that I'm getting mist on my face and the somebody who bumped into me is saying, "Well, my my, look who it is." That's when I look up and get the shock of my life: it's Mrs. Lindop.

Mrs. Heather Lindop.

Ernest Lindop's mother.

She waves a lettuce in my face. "Hi, Jake. Remember me?"

That's when I did it—The Gulp.

Until something like this happens to you, you'll never know how long a swallow can take. When I was finally able to talk, I said, "Uh . . . hi. . . ."

Brilliant, huh?

Her smile was so big it bumped into her hoop earrings. "So how's it going, Jake? Haven't seen you guys lately. Where ya been?"

"Oh, around," I said.

I couldn't believe she wasn't clobbering me with the lettuce and kicking me in the shins.

"Ernie misses you," she said.

It took awhile to sink in.

Ernie misses you.

I thought, *Is it possible? He didn't tell her what I said?*

"Especially since what happened," she said.

I did a mini gulp. "What was that?" I said.

"Oh, somebody knocked down Ernie's clubhouse." She pitched the lettuces into her cart. "Haven't you seen?"

"No," I lied. "We were on vacation."

"Who would *do* such a thing?" she said. I was going to answer something like "Beats me," but I saw that she wasn't really asking *me*, she was looking around the ceiling. She was asking the universe. Her eyes came back to me. "So Ernie was pretty sad there for a while."

That's not all he was sad about.

"But then"—her face and her voice got peppy again—"you know Ernie. He bounces back. So now he's busy rebuilding."

She was looking hard at me now, and for some weird reason I knew exactly what she wanted me to say. So I said it. "Good."

She nodded. She squeezed my shoulder. "Y'know, I shouldn't tell you this, because Ernie likes all of you. But"—her voice got whispery, she leaned in— "you're his favorite, Jake. He likes you best."

He never told her!

I heard my mouth saying, "I like him too."

"And the strangest thing," she said. "Guess what somebody did?"

"What?"

"Somebody left one of those leveler thingies in the hut, that carpenters use." She laughed. "I guess they couldn't stand to see the lopsided walls anymore!"

We both laughed.

Lily

It's a playground!

Well, the start of a playground.

Only two days later and here's what we have:

- a basketball and hoop
- a swing set
- a pipe

The Addisons bought the ball and hoop and set it up. It's only five feet high, still way too high for Devon to dunk. But he loves to try—when he can get the ball away from Sydney and me.

The swing set came from my backyard. Jake and I haven't used it for years, but it was still sitting there. Devon won't let anybody push him.

The pipe. It's plastic. Black. Thirty-six inches across. My parents got it from a friend who's laying a storm sewer. They had ten feet of pipe left over. All my parents had to do was haul it here on the truck and smooth out the edges. It's perfect—and irresistible—for a little kid to crawl through. Not to mention his big-girl babysitters, who he orders to play the parts of monsters or T. rexes or man-eating crocs chasing him through the Tunnel of Doom.

Devon hasn't asked to go to McDonald's in two days.

Jake

Lily's voice. "Wake up." She was shaking me. "Wake *up*."

"Huh? . . . Wha—?"

"There's somebody downstairs. He wants you."

"Who?"

"*I* don't know." She dragged me out of bed, pushed me. "Go."

I staggered down the stairs in my underwear. I figured I was still asleep because I dreamed Ernest Lindop was standing in my living room.

"Hi, Jake," he said. He grabbed my hand and shook it.

It wasn't a dream hand. It was real.

He looked me over. "I sleep in my underwear too," he said. I've never seen such a big smile so early in the morning.

The voice in my head was saying, *Why are you here? To hit me? You hate me.* But all that came out was, "Hffffgg."

He laughed. "Sorry I got you out of bed. I can come back later."

"'Sokay," I said.

"I just wanted to thank you." Was this a joke? I just stared. He was carrying a plastic bag. He pulled something out of it. "For this." It was the carpenter's level. He was staring, his face tilting into mine. "It *was* you, wasn't it?"

I nodded. How did he know?

He nodded. "Thought so. My mother saw somebody running away from the porch the other night. She thought it might be you." He laughed. "I didn't even know what it was. My dad had to tell me. So"—he gave me a little arm punch—"thanks to you, I can make straight walls."

This was crazy. I'd confessed to trashing his shack, and now he was *thanking* me? I couldn't think of a thing to say.

Suddenly he was looking at me all serious. "Jake?" he said.

"Huh?" I said.

He took a deep breath, like he was pumping himself up to speak. "Jake, did you *really* bust up my clubhouse?"

I've never been stared at so hard. I couldn't lie. "No," I said.

He screeched. He fist-bumped himself. "I *knew* it! The more I thought about it, the more I couldn't believe it was really you. Why did you say you did it?"

I was starting to feel stupid, standing there in my underwear. "Do I have to answer that?"

He tried to sound like a drill sergeant, which was pretty funny coming from him. "It's a command, private."

Now it was my turn to take a deep breath. "So Bump wouldn't beat you up," I said.

"So I was right. It *was* Bump who did it."

I nodded.

"And you . . . you saved me from Bump."

I nodded.

"You didn't think I could beat him up?"

I didn't know what to say, and suddenly he was hugging me. Ernest Lindop was laughing and hugging me in my own living room. And a tiny dark voice was saying, *Holy Death Rays—you're being hugged by a supergoober!*

Lily

Sydney's family went to Ocean City for the day. They asked me to go along. We had a great time. The boardwalk. The beach. The waves. Ice-cream waffles. Which explains why we didn't know what happened until late in the day.

On the drive home Devon kept pestering his father to stop at Devon Park, which is what we now call the playground. Devon's dad said it was too late to play outside, but he would at least drive by to take a look at it. Sydney's parents hadn't seen it yet.

When we pulled up to Devon Park, we got one of the all-time shockers. Somebody had painted something on the Tunnel of Doom—the word GOOBERS in yellow letters against the black pipe.

"Vandals," said Mr. Dodds.

Before he finished the word I was out of the car and racing for the pipe. The letters were big and sloppy, and somehow that made it even worse.

Devon was right behind me. He touched the paint. He didn't seem very upset. He turned to me. "What's it say, Lil-wee? Devon Park?"

"Yeah," I said. "Devon Park."

I figured, why tell him the truth? But it back-fired. He started to wail. "But it's messy! Look how messy it is!"

By now everybody was at the pipe, including Mrs. Addison. She was sad-faced. "I didn't see it till noon," she said. "We were hoping to get it painted over before you all saw it."

Devon had already forgotten it. He dived into the pipe, popped out the other end, and cried, "Basketball!"

Mrs. Addison brought out the ball. While the others were shooting baskets with Devon, I noticed something on the ground by the pipe. A black blob. Looked kind of like tar, but I had a feeling it wasn't. The sun was down behind the houses. It was getting dark. Mr. Dodds was lifting Devon for a slam dunk. I knew what I should do, but it was too gross to even think about. Then I thought, *The Gray Shadow would do it.*

I picked up the black blob. Even in the dim light I could see it had a chewed-up look. I brought it to my nose. I sniffed.

I was right.

Jake

I didn't want to hurt his feelings, so I let the hug go on for as long as he wanted. Finally it ended.

"How did you know where I live?" I asked him.

He said he bumped into Nacho and Burke and he asked them.

As he watched me eat breakfast, he said thanking me wasn't the only reason he came over. "I'd like you to help me build the clubhouse," he said.

Right then I realized I had been hoping he would ask. "Sure," I said.

He high-fived himself. "Yes!"

On the bike ride to his house he said, "I was just thinking something."

"What?" I said.

"Maybe we should get some more help. Maybe

we should ask Nacho and Burke. What do you think?"

I guess he knew better than to ask Bump. As for the other two, I tried to think of a good reason why not, but I couldn't. "Good idea," I said.

I led Ernie to the hideout. The guys weren't there, but Ernie was hyper-impressed by the umbrella tree. He walked in circles under the leafy dome. "Wow. . . cool," he kept saying.

We bumped into them five minutes later on the road. The shock on their faces was priceless, seeing me with Ernie, but they quick switched to cool. "Hey, dudes," I said.

"Hi, Nacho. Hi, Burke," said Ernie, his usual cheery self. "I found Jake"—he laughed—"as you can see. Thanks again for the address. And I know Bump did it. Jake told me his confession was fake."

The guys looked at me. I nodded. "It's all cool."

I could see them relax. Their faces changed. Their eyes. They were no longer looking at a goober. Or, even if they were, they didn't care. Each of them reached out and fist-bumped Ernie. He was beaming.

We headed for Meeker Street. As we got closer

to his house, Ernie started laughing. It was just a chuckle at first, and by the time we hit his driveway it was a howl.

"What's so funny?" said Nacho.

Ernie wiped away laugh tears with his shirttail. "My clubhouse. It's leaning more than the tower of Pisa. It's probably the ugliest clubhouse ever!"

He cracked up again, and the rest of us joined in.

First I raced back to my house for more tools, while the others raided the garage for Mr. Lindop's tools. We started by tearing down the mess Ernie had already made. When his mom came out, she knew without asking what we were doing. "Thank you, boys!" she called, and went back inside. We could hear her laughing all morning.

Mrs. Lindop fed us lunch. It was maybe the best lunch I ever had. Not because of the food but because of—I don't know how to say it—the fun. The laughs. The talk. The good feelings. The guys. The sun streaming in through the lemony curtains.

Maybe it was the light that gave me the idea. As we were building a wall after lunch, I said, "Why don't we put in a window?"

Everybody thought it was a great idea.

"But we don't know how to put in a window," said Burke.

"My parents do," I said.

At dinner I asked Mom and Dad if they could help us make a clubhouse for my new friend. They said sure, they can do it day after tomorrow, which is Saturday.

My head is spinning with all the stuff that's happened since Lily shook me awake this morning. If I had to pick the best day ever, I think this would be it.

Lily

I'm usually groggy when I wake up in the morning. Not today. I opened my eyes, dropped to the floor, reached under the bed, and pulled out my Gray Shadow Crimestoppers kit. I looked at my Gray Shadow hat. Should I wear it? No, I decided. That's for play. I'm not playing today. I took out the only two things I needed: handcuffs and whistle.

I had to practice. I snuck into Jake's room. He was still sleeping. His arm was hanging off the bed. Perfect. I knelt by the bed. I opened one cuff. I snapped it over his wrist, clicked it shut. Took maybe three seconds. He squawked. His cuffed arm flew up and caught me in the lip. He stared at the cuff, stared at me, shoved me onto my butt. "Get this off me!"

"I have the key," I said, all calm. "Say please or you'll be wearing that thing all day long."

He started to get out of bed, real slow, the way Mom moves when it's don't-even-think-about-it time. Things were instantly obvious:

He wasn't going to say please.

He was going to kill me.

I pulled the key from my pocket and unlocked him and got outta there. I tasted something. My lip was bleeding. I got a wad of toilet paper and clamped it between my lips.

But I was happy. The practice pinch had gone pretty good. I practiced some more on my old Nerf bat. Each time I snapped the handcuff on the bat, I pictured Bump Stubbins's wrist.

I was ready.

I was too excited to eat breakfast. I put on my watch, got my bike, and headed off. But I couldn't go straight to his house. It was too early. He's a lazy bum, so I knew he wouldn't be up and out very early. I figured nine a.m. was about right.

I cruised the streets, passing time. *Exposure.* That was my weapon. Not a stun gun or nightstick. Most criminals are sneaky, my Crimestoppers manual says. *They do their dark deeds in the concealing shadows of law-abiding society,* the manual says. What many criminals fear most is *the blinding beam of justice* lighting up their creepy little crannies and showing other people what scumbags they are. Exposure works especially good on criminals with a conscience. I wasn't sure if Bump Stubbins had a conscience, but I figured it was worth a try. Not to mention that he was bigger than me now, so I couldn't just beat him up like I did when he smashed my snow fort.

The sun was warm on my bare knees. I checked my watch. 8:55. Time!

I pulled into his driveway. 129 Mulberry.

Across the street I could see kids popping up and down behind a high hedge. Trampoline.

Up the street a lady with a pink sunshade was on her knees in a flower garden.

A teenage boy was looking down at his dog, waiting, pooper-scooper bag ready.

A UPS man was lugging a big box up a driveway.

Good. I wanted people. Witnesses.

I rang the doorbell. I kept ringing it. He was probably still in bed. He probably figured if he didn't come down and answer it, the bell ringer would go away.

I must have been ringing for five minutes before the door finally opened. He wore sweat shorts. That was all. His toes curled under his feet so he looked toeless. His eyes were sleepy slits. I could see him struggle to bring my face into focus. When he did, the eyes came open and I could practically hear them speak: *What the heck is* she *doing here?*

When the moment arrives, don't delay, the manual says. The best time to pinch a perp is when they're *confused or otherwise distracted*.

"Hold out your hand," I said. I said it like a command, no-nonsense, like he had no choice. *Your voice is your authority.*

Sure enough, the dummy held out his hand. *Snap!* I had the cuff on him. Before he could say, "Huh?" I had the other cuff on my own wrist.

"You're under arrest," I told him.

He blinked. He stared at his wrist. He was finally waking up. "You can't arrest me. You're not a cop."

"Citizen's arrest," I said.

He blinked. "Huh?"

"Vandalizing the playground. Painting GOOBERS on the pipe."

"What're you talking about?" He was getting growly now. He was remembering he's bigger than me. "I didn't do nuthin." He yanked his cuffed hand away—which yanked me lurching right into him. My head clipped his chin. For the first time he realized he was handcuffed to me.

I took the plastic Baggie from my pocket. In the Baggie was the chewed-up glob of black licorice. I wagged it in front of his face. *Hard evidence wins the case.* "This was found at the scene of the crime." I smiled.

He tugged at the handcuff. He hollered. "Take this off!"

The Crimestopper must remain calm, alert, and in control.

"I will," I said calmly. "When you fix the damage you did."

He let out a screech with no particular word attached to it. He threw out his cuffed arm, which made me slap myself in the face. Maybe I should have handcuffed him to my leg. He tried to stomp back inside the house and almost slammed the door on his own arm. His face was raging purple. I hadn't seen him so mad since the time I struck him out in Pee Wee Baseball. He screamed in my face: "Forget it, girlie!"

I stayed in control. "Forget it?" I shook my head calmly. "I don't think so."

The unexpected is your friend.

Without warning I yanked him out of the doorway and onto the porch. I pulled the whistle from my pocket. I looked at him. I smiled. "Forget it?" I pulled him to the top step. I faced the street. "Forget it, *girlie*?"

I blew the whistle.

Nothing else sounds like a whistle. You expect it on a basketball court or football field—but not on a nice quiet street with flower beds and dog walkers.

Mulberry Street froze. The UPS truck jerked to a stop. The pink sunshade turned. The trampolining kids boggled for two pops above the hedge, then reappeared in full bodies on the sidewalk. Even the dog stopped in its tracks to stare at me.

"HEY, EVERYBODY!" I yelled. "BUMP STUBBINS WRECKS LITTLE KIDS'

PLAYGROUNDS! BUMP STUB—"

A hand mashed my mouth shut. Bump hauled me by my cuffed wrist across the porch and into the house. His eyes were wild. He was panting. *Well well, he has a conscience*, I thought. "Okay," he gasped, "okay."

I took off the cuffs. My mouth and my whistle were all the shackles I needed now.

Exposure.

I let him go upstairs to put on more clothes. He got his bike. We rode to Devon Park.

Along the way I suddenly realized I had given all my attention to pinching the perp. Now what?

Mrs. Addison was a big help. She drove us to the paint store and laid out the plan. Except for feeding us lunch, she stayed behind the scenes for the rest of the day.

One coat of black, and GOOBERS was gone. Then came the new name as big and yellow as before. And better. Turned out the perp could be really neat if he tried. Thanks to quick-dry paint, the job was done way before dinnertime. Now the lettering said:

TUNNEL OF DOOM

Jake

If my parents weren't builders, I guess I never would have heard of barn raising. It happens with Amish people. If somebody needs a new barn, all the nearby farmers come over and build the guy a new barn all in one day. I guess what happened today was a clubhouse raising.

My parents wanted to start at seven a.m. Seven a.m. to my parents is like ten a.m. to normal people. As we pulled into the driveway, I could hardly believe what I saw: the Lindops—Mr., Mrs., Ernie—all waiting and waving on the porch. But the biggest surprise was Lily—she came along. And nobody made her. She hasn't been grumpy for the last couple days. She's talking to me again.

Mr. Lindop went for supplies. Dad set up his

workbench in the yard. He ran a long orange cord to an outlet on the porch and connected the buzz saw.

Then we started building. It was hot. Mrs. Lindop brought out lemonade and iced tea with mint leaves in it.

After a while Nacho and Burke showed up, still half asleep. Their main jobs were to stay out of the way.

By lunchtime the walls were up and spaces framed for two windows and a door. Mrs. Lindop had a picnic set up in the shade of the back porch. Cold cuts. Potato rolls. Chicken salad. Blue corn chips. Pickles. Olives stuffed with cheese. Brownies. Watermelon. You name it. Once, as I looked up from my sandwich, I saw Bump ride by.

All afternoon we were swimming in sweat. Everybody was dragging but Ernie. He was darting like a squirrel. I swear, from seven a.m. till the end, I never saw the smile leave his face.

By dinnertime the job was almost done. Peaked roof with shingles. Hardwood floor. It was beautiful.

"I want to live here," I said, only half joking.

Last came the paint. "What color, Ernie?" said my dad.

Ernie didn't hesitate. "Orange!" Everybody made groany smiles. Before anyone could say, *You can't paint a clubhouse orange*, Dad said, "Orange it is."

An hour later, one wall to a painter, it was done. A miniature orange house. "I take it back," I said. "I *don't* want to live here." Everybody laughed— Ernie loudest of all. I've never seen anybody so happy as that kid.

"One last thing," my dad said. He went to the truck and came back with a weather vane he had saved from an old job. He screwed it onto the roof. It was a floppy-eared dog with its straight-out tail pointing in the wind direction.

Then we all went out for pizza to celebrate.

Lily

It was Poppy's idea for me to help build the clubhouse.

Here's how it happened.

I couldn't wait to tell Poppy about my detective work and citizen's arrest and the new paint job. Telling it was almost as much fun as doing it.

As I was blabbing on, I noticed him grinning at the bowl of fudge ripple ice cream in front of me. I looked down. It was a creamy puddle. We laughed. "Guess I got carried away," I said.

Now he was aiming his smile at me. I asked him what else was funny.

"Not funny," he said. "Just nice."

"What's nice?"

"Something's missing," he said. "Do you know what?"

"Tell me."

"You haven't mentioned Jake or goombla this whole time."

I thought about it. He was right.

"In fact," he said, "I don't think I've heard those words since you've been telling me about your days with your new friend Sydney."

"So what are you saying?" I asked him.

He took away the puddle bowl and brought me another with three new scoops. "I'm saying I think you've done it."

I knew exactly what he meant, but I wanted to hear it in his words. "Yeah? What'd I do?"

"You got a life. You're a new Lily. You learned that you could go solo, stand on your own without clinging to your brother."

I took a spoonful of fudge ripple. I nodded. "Yeah. I guess you're right."

He stared at me, thinking. "How would you like to *know*, not guess?"

I shrugged. "Sure."

"That clubhouse I heard about? That Jake and your parents are going to rebuild for Jake's new friend, kid named Ernie?"

"Yeah," I said. "What about it?"

"I'm thinking maybe you should jump in. Help them build it."

"Why should I?" I said. "It's gonna be for Jake and his friends. *His* life."

He snapped his fingers. "That's the point. It would be a good test for you. Prove to yourself that you can spend a day with your brother—with the *boys*—and walk away on your own two feet. Still the new Lily." He took the spoon out of my hand and stole a big gob of my ice cream. "Whaddaya think? You gonna do it? Or wimp out? Afraid you can't pass the test?"

I didn't wimp out.

Next morning I rode the family truck to Meeker Street. I sweated. Lifted. Hammered. Ate. Talked. Even laughed at their stupid jokes. Nacho. Burke. Ernie. Jake. The boys. I asked myself, *Do I still want to be one of them?* The answer was no. I prayed they didn't remember that day I yelled after them from my bike, "I'm not a girl!"

The day came and went, and at the end of it I was still me. Still standing on my own two feet. The new Lily. I passed the test.

Jake

The door was open. The two windows were open. Still it was hot in the clubhouse. But we didn't care. We sat on folding chairs—Ernie, me, Burke, Nacho. Our lemonades sat on a TV tray, along with a bowl of munchies that Ernie's mom kept coming in to refill. She was funny. Every time she came, she knocked on the door and said, "May a lowly female have permission to enter the grand palace of major dudes?" Ernie acted all serious and granted her permission, then said, "Females are welcome, Mom."

We sat and munched and talked and just chilled out in the coolest clubhouse in town. We talked a lot about school, which starts next week. Then Ernie said, "Let's play Revelation. You have to tell something about yourself that the rest of us don't know."

We said okay. Nacho went first. He told about the time in third grade when he sang "God Bless America" for the class and everybody was laughing because his fly was open.

Burke told about the time he cut a bug in half. That was years ago and he just remembered it the other day and he really feels bad about it.

I took a deep breath and told them about the first sleepwalk to the train station. Their mouths and eyes were gaping. When I finished, I never heard such silence in my life. Finally Ernie reached over and touched my arm. "You're lucky," he said.

Nobody said anything else. We were waiting for Ernie's revelation. It took awhile before we realized he had already started. He was holding out his hand, palm up. In the middle was a mark. Round. Smaller than a dime. Whitish. I wondered why he was showing us.

"Blister?" I said, remembering our blister lies.

He shook his head, still smiling.

"So, what?" said Nacho.

"Scar," said Ernie.

And then he told us. Back at his last school in Gary, Indiana, there was a kid who zeroed in on him. The kid would trip him and knock his books to the ground and make life miserable for him. The kid was already smoking, and one day he shoved Ernie up against a wall and said, "I heard you been bad-mouthin' me." Which of course Ernie wasn't, but the kid was just setting him up. "I'll teach ya to bad-mouth me," the kid says, and he grabs Ernie's hand and snuffs out his lit cigarette right there in the palm.

"One day you asked me why we moved away from Gary and came here," he said. "That's why."

"I don't blame you for leaving that dump," said Burke.

"It wasn't my choice," said Ernie. "My parents made me. I tried to hide the burn, but it got infected and the school nurse saw it and sent me to the hospital, and that's when my parents found out."

I was shocked. "You mean, after all that, you didn't *want* to move?"

Ernie shook his head. "I had friends. Most of the kids were nice." He laughed. "I wasn't going to let one rotten apple run me outta town!"

We all clinked glasses and drank to that and I thought, *Goobers have guts.*

"But," Ernie said, holding up his finger, "that doesn't mean I'm sorry. Because if we didn't move, I never would have met you guys." He was doing it again, smiling and hard-staring each of us.

I swallowed. I clinked his glass. "We're glad too, Ernie."

Ernie took a swig. "I'll tell you, it was coming down to the wire. I was getting nervous at the prospect of starting a new school without having a single friend."

"Now you have three," said Nacho.

"Right," said Ernie. "Too bad it's not four." We knew who he was referring to. "I guess Bump is busy looking for more goobers."

I almost gagged on my mouthful of corn chips. For a minute you could practically hear the ice melting in the lemonade. Sooner or later somebody had to say something. I swallowed. "He's prob'ly away on vacation."

"Or maybe"— he snapped his fingers—"he just can't bring himself to be friends with a goober."

"Why do you keep saying that?" said Burke.

"You're not a goober," said Nacho.

"Sure I am," said Ernie. He looked proud. He laughed. "Whatever it is." He looked at me. "What exactly makes a goober a goober, anyway?"

Dead silence.

I finally choked out, "You guys are all so stupid. There's no such thing as goobers."

Ernie just smiled. Then chuckled. "And I bet Soop doesn't really mean 'cool,' does it?"

More silence. *Enough of this*, I thought. "Hey," I said, "anybody going out for football this year?"

Lily

Sydney slept over last night. She was everything Anna Matuzak was not. No makeup. No adoring herself in the mirror. No hogging the pizza or the bed space. No complaining.

But lots of burping. We had a contest. She won. I was laughing too hard to care about losing.

We spent a couple hours in the Cool-It Room. Armed with markers. There's no empty space left on the walls.

She saw every nook and cranny of the house except the basement. A couple days ago my dad installed a lock on the basement door. He won't tell me why, only that if I'm dumb enough to break through and go down, I do so on pain of death. I told him I better not be locked out for long because my train stuff is down there.

We wound up watching TV from the bed and eating M&M's. The last time I looked at the clock it said 1:30 a.m. I guess we scared Jake away. He spent the night at Poppy's.

We were zombies heading over to Sydney's house this morning to pick up Devon for the day. He usually wants to head straight for the playground. Not today. He wanted to hang out at my house. Jealous about Sydney's overnight, I guess.

One thing happened that drained some of the juice out of our super-great overnight.

Devon hid in the mudroom closet. No big deal, except we thought he was lost. Maybe unconscious. Maybe wandering down the street. Maybe whatever. We called and called. No answer. Sydney was frantic, ready to cry, when we found him all grinny in the closet.

The whole thing made me a little sad. It reminded me of the times when Jake and I couldn't play hide-and-seek because we always knew where each other was.

Jake

I slept over at Poppy's last night. Lily was having her new best pal overnight, so I escaped.

Or at least I thought I escaped. Until I had the dream. I'm standing in the open, just me and an empty blue sky, and I look up and I see Lily falling. She's coming from really high, like above the blue, but I know instantly that she's coming right down on me, and I hold out my arms and I catch her and she laughs and laughs. She won't stop laughing.

Lily

Sydney and Devon got shipped off to her uncle Bob's for a couple days, so this morning I biked over to Poppy's. I love having keys to two houses. We're having a heat wave, but Poppy's house is always cool.

At times like this I wish he didn't work all day, but at least he's got Wii now. I talked him into it. We do sword fights and Ping-Pong and stuff. It's not as much fun by myself, but it's okay. The only thing I don't like is that it's hard to cheat with Wii. I did some bowling for a while, then beat myself in tennis.

I made a sardine sandwich with onion and mustard. Poppy says it's a big world, I need to try new stuff. Then I headed to the basement to play darts. It occurred to me to go out back and weed Poppy's flower garden. It's his least favorite job. I was torn, because I wanted to do it and surprise him, but I'm terrified of that big black devil dog in the next yard.

I looked out the back window. I didn't see the dog. I opened the back door and peeked. No dog. I slunk into the yard, ready to bolt back in. No dog. I pulled as many weeds as I could hold in two hands and ran back inside.

TV was boring. Every channel. I was starting to talk to myself. I kept thinking about Jake telling me I should come over to the orange clubhouse. On the TV a cartoon dog was chasing a cartoon squirrel around a cartoon tree. "That's it," I said out loud. I clicked off the TV. I missed Sydney. I was so bored I was ready to look up Anna Matuzak.

I must have backed out the front door, because when I pulled it shut and turned around, I found myself staring at the devil dog. He was sitting at the foot of the porch steps, right next to my bike. A bird was chirping somewhere and the street was all sunny and nice, but my world stopped at the beast. Then I heard something that wasn't the bird

chirping. It was so low I didn't realize
it was. Then I did. It was the dog.
hard to explain, but a low, soft growl
rifying than a roar. I never got so mu
in my life as I did from those two littl
They didn't blink, only stared. The bi
never moved. And neither did I. I froz
had to pee. I clenched up. Poppy's fro
automatically when you close it. The k
pocket. But I knew that if I so much
finger, the monster would be leaping

Jake

Another scorcher. It was probably hotter in the clubhouse than outside, but we didn't want to leave. Besides lemonade, Mrs. L was bringing us homemade ice-cube Popsicles—grape and orange.

We had our shirts off, except for Ernie. He's no scrawnier than the rest of us. Just more modest, I guess.

We were talking about school starting soon and all the usual junk, but my mind was on a different track from my mouth. I kept looking at Ernie, with his Daffy Duck T-shirt and his white smear of sunblock on his sunburned nose and his clumsiness and his never-ending cheeriness, and I realized he was the same as always. He fit the definition of a goober as perfectly as ever. He hadn't changed at all. *I* had. *We* had. Forget what I said a couple pages ago: goobers *do* exist. They are what they are, which is pretty much what I thought they were. What Bump thinks they are. But Bump is missing the point: it's *okay* to be a goober. Beneath every goober is a kid. A person. Maybe he's not what you would call "regular." But so what? Is that a bad thing? Turns out goobers—this goober, anyway—make great friends. I'll take a goober over a Death Ray any day.

The guys were talking about school activities, and Ernie was saying he wanted to join the band and learn to play the trombone. As he was demonstrating trombone playing he knocked his lemonade off the TV tray. As he dove for his falling glass he knocked over the others. We all laughed and got down on our knees, and as I was picking an ice cube off the new hardwood floor I had a sudden feeling. It had nothing to do with ice cubes or lemonade or friends or clubhouses. It had to do with my sister. Lily. I can't describe it except to say that for the first time in a long time that special sense was back, what we used to call goombla. If the wordless feeling could speak, it would have whispered, *She needs you.*

Next thing I knew, I was flying down the streets on my bike and busting into Poppy's driveway. The big black dog from next door was blocking the front steps. Just sitting there. Lily was on the porch. She looked like a statue, like some alien paralyzer ray had zapped her.

The dog didn't bother to get up when he saw me. He just swung his big black head. I knew he lived next door, and I knew Lily was terrified of him, even though Poppy keeps telling her he's just "a big baby." The dog barked at me. I have to admit it didn't sound like a friendly bark. More like a don't-come-one-inch-closer bark. Then the dog got up on all fours. He barked at me some more. His head bounced with every bark like a recoiling pistol. *This dog wants to kill me*, I thought. I don't know how long I stood there, staring back and forth from the dog to Lily. Then I was aware of two things: I was moving, and I was thinking, *I'm gonna die.* And then the dog was coming at me and its bark was different and it was jumping up at me and licking my face and I knew Poppy was right, it *was* just a big baby.

Lily was still on the porch, still frozen. I went to her. Her eyes were horror-movie wide. I cupped her shoulders. "It's okay," I said. She flinched—the dog was licking her hand. Then I felt her relax. Tears came. She sagged into me.

Her voice was muffled against my shirt. "You *knew*, didn't you?"

"Yeah," I said, "I knew."

Lily

Devon Park is going public!

Devon finally got tired of having a playground all to himself. He whined to Mrs. Addison: "I want playmates!"

The Addisons are giving him more than playmates. They've added a sandbox and sliding board to the playground.

We made a sign:

GRAND OPENING SATURDAY!

DEVON PARK PLAYGROUND

(little kids only)

I went to tell Poppy all about it today. There was a monster in the kitchen. The cantaloupe. Right where it's been for half the summer.

Is there a word for worse-than-rotten? It was soft and moldy. Poppy pressed a finger into it. It made a glurpy sound. I hung back by the fridge. My stomach was looking for a way out.

"I told you," said Poppy. "You can turn your back on it. Ignore it. Forget it. But it's still here. Right where you left it. Just like your goombla."

"My goombla isn't sickening," I pointed out.

Before I could stop him, he pulled his new long knife from the drawer and sliced the cantaloupe in half. One look at the smelly orange mush, one whiff, and I was outta there. Let somebody else tell him about Devon Park.

"Hey!" he called. "How about some ice cream? Fudge ripple!"

I charged out the front door. "No thanks," I called. "Not hungry."

Jake

Mom and Dad took me to the grand opening of Lily's friend's little brother's new playground. They wouldn't tell me why. Nacho and Burke and Ernie were there too. Everybody was staring at a big humpy something under a tarp. When Mom and Dad whipped off the tarp, I suddenly knew why I was there and what Dad had been working on in the basement. It was a wooden locomotive. Red and blue and silver. Letters running from headlamp to engineer's cab said CALIFORNIA ZEPHYR.

My parents held off the swarming little kids so my sister and I could sit in the cab first. Lily was crying. I might have too, if I was a girl.

"It's our dream train," she said.

"Our birthday train," I said.

I closed my eyes. I was back in the Moffat Tunnel. I could hear the click of train wheels.

Lily poked me. She was grinning. "Smell anything?"

I sniffed. "Pickles!"

We laughed.

I told her I was sorry I missed our birthday sleepwalk at the train station. I told her if it would make her feel better she could punch me one time to make up for it. She did.

I invited her to come to the new clubhouse. She said she has better things to do. I told her Bump is gone. I told her we're not the Death Rays anymore. She could bring Sydney and Devon. She said why would she want to hang out with a bunch of boys. I reminded her that a couple months ago she said she wasn't a girl. She punched me again.

The next day we tried to play hide-and-seek. We couldn't.

Lily said "I ate them" before I could say "Where are my pumpkin seeds?"

It looks like we're back on track.

And it feels like the end of this book, so

Lily

Not so fast, buster.

Before we wrap this thing up, one thing's gonna change. I don't want to hear you tell me one more time—ever!—that you're older than me.

Jake

It's only eleven minutes.

Lily

Feels like eleven years. As long as you have a death grip on the Big Eleven, I'm never going to feel really equal. So give them up. All eleven minutes. *Now.*

Jake

Okay. But only if you stop stealing my pumpkin seeds. Deal?

Lily

Deal.

Okay . . . so let's do the last chapter together, since now we're finally, really, truly, totally equal

Jake

sister-approved

Jake and Lily

twins!

JERRY SPINELLI received the Newbery Medal for MANIAC MAGEE and a Newbery Honor for WRINGER. His other books include SMILES TO GO, LOSER, SPACE STATION SEVENTH GRADE, WHO PUT THAT HAIR IN MY TOOTHBRUSH?, DUMP DAYS, and STARGIRL. His novels are recognized for their humor and poignancy, and his characters and situations are often drawn from his real-life experience as a father of six children. Jerry lives with his wife, Eileen, also a writer, in Wayne, Pennsylvania. You can visit him online at www.jerryspinelli.com.